Cambridgeshire Libraries, Archives and Information Service

This book is due for return on or before the latest date shown above but may be renewed up to three times unless it has been requested by another customer.

Books can be renewed –
in person at your local library

Cambridgeshire
County Council

Online www.cambridgeshire.gov.uk/library

Please note that charges are made on overdue books.

Emba Oak and the Beckoning Bones
An original concept by author Jenny Moore
© Jenny Moore, 2023

Cover artwork by David Dean
© David Dean, 2023

Published by MAVERICK ARTS PUBLISHING LTD
Studio 11, City Business Centre, 6 Brighton Road,
Horsham, West Sussex, RH13 5BB
+44 (0) 1403 256941
© Maverick Arts Publishing Limited April 2023

First edition April 2023

A CIP catalogue record for this book is available
at the British Library.

ISBN: 978-1-84886-949-3

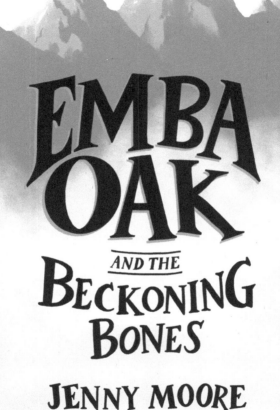

EMBA OAK

AND THE
BECKONING BONES

JENNY MOORE

To Dafydd, Lucy and Dan,

with love xx

(Not Quite) Chapter 1

The Heroically Happy Homecoming

All the best homecomings start with a warm, welcoming light in the distance, beckoning weary travellers back, and the smell of cooked food carried on the breeze like a promise. And all the best homecomings *end* with a full stomach and a nice, cosy bed. Ah yes, bed… Emba Oak had dreamt of nothing but bed (and dinner) as she trudged through the darkening woods with Fred and Odolf towards the cave she called home. Defeating her dragon-obsessed father, Necromalcolm, had proved to be tiring work. As had the three-day trek home again afterwards. At least they were nearly back now.

Almost there, Emba told herself for the two-hundred-and-eighteenth time in a row, imagining the freshly lit fire they'd soon be warming themselves at. A freshly lit fire with a steaming pot of squirrel stew bubbling away over the flames... Wait, no. The *last* thing Emba wanted to think about was a bubbling pot. It reminded her of the terrible look on Necromalcolm's face as he'd tumbled back into his own cauldron. It reminded her of the lizard Odolf claimed to have seen scuttling out of the same cauldron after it was all over. Except it wasn't all over, was it? Not if there really *had* been a lizard. Not if the lizard had been Necromalcolm, slinking away into the shadows to regain his strength for a fresh attack...

No, no, no. Emba pushed the image away again. She wasn't going to spoil her long-awaited return to the cave with worries about Necromalcolm. This was supposed to be their heroic homecoming... A homecoming with blisters and rumbling bellies, admittedly, but heroic all the same. And like all the best homecomings, this one came with a warm, welcoming light in the distance—a bright orangey light coming from the cave entrance, calling the weary travellers back.

Hang on, Emba thought with a sudden jolt. What was a light doing in the cave if no one was there?

That wasn't a welcome, she realised. It was a warning. Just like the giant, red crack that had suddenly appeared in the sky overhead.

Oh no. Not again.

[Proper] Chapter 1

The Horrendously Horrible Homecoming

"Wait," Emba hissed at the others, "there's someone in the cave. Look!"

She pointed towards the light. *Two* lights, in fact. They looked almost like eyes—giant, unblinking eyes burning in the darkness—but then the eyes began to move, shifting from one direction to the other as if they were searching for something. Or someone. They weren't eyes, they were lanterns.

"You're right," said Fred, with a wheezing gasp. "Get down."

Emba and Odolf dropped into a low crouch behind a nearby rock, while Fred settled for hunching her head even lower over her chest. Her crouching days were over, thanks to the painful stiffness in her 'old, aching bones' as she liked to call them.

"Shouldn't we be trying to *protect* the cave, instead of hiding?" said Odolf. "What if they're after the Tome of Terrible Tomorrows? What if the prophecy falls into the wrong hands?"

Emba guessed he was thinking about the Final Prophecy. Odolf was *always* thinking about the Final Prophecy, which foretold the saving of a kingdom by 'a hero forged in fiercest flame, a child of iron and pain'. Odolf was convinced that he was the hero in question, and that his magically protective belt buckle was the key to fulfilling his heroic destiny. There was just one teeny tiny problem with that. The belt buckle didn't actually belong to Odolf. He'd stolen it from the duchess while he was working as a castle blacksmith, before she could give it to Necromalcolm for his birthday. And now there was a new, slightly larger problem too. The magic belt buckle was currently in the possession of some horse thieves, who'd stolen it from Odolf on the way to the castle. That's unless they'd already sold it on, in which case it could be anywhere by now.

"Hush now, Odolf," said Fred, her left eye twitching as she placed a steadying hand on his shoulder. Her eye always twitched when she was worried. "Let's not do anything rash. If they're after the Tome, we're probably too late already," she told him. "And if they're after *us*, then the last thing we want to do is go charging in there without a plan."

"So, what *is* the plan?" asked Odolf.

Fred's left eye twitched harder. "I don't know," she admitted. "Let's lie low for a bit and see what happens."

Emba hoped that whatever was going to happen happened quickly. Being so close to home and yet still so far from a fire and food, and bed, was almost too much to bear. She'd been looking forward to using the 'chamber pot' as well, even if it *was* only an old tin bucket. A tin bucket was luxury compared to weeing in bushes and patches of stinging nettles, which is what she'd spent the entire journey from Necromalcolm's tower doing. Well, not the whole journey obviously, only the bits where her bladder needed emptying. But Emba's bladder would just have to wait, along with the rest of her.

"Look," she said at last. "I think they're going."

Yes, the lanterns—and the lantern bearers, presumably—were heading away from the cave now. Whoever they were, and whatever they were looking for, they were gone. But the red crack in the sky was still there, which wasn't a good sign. On the contrary, it was usually a sign of terrible danger waiting just around the corner. Emba still wasn't sure what the crack *was* exactly—some kind of fissure or tear between the earthly realm and the dragon realm perhaps—but what she *did* know was that no one else could see it. She knew she ought to tell Fred. It was the sort of thing Fred would want to know. But that might delay their homecoming even further, and Emba really, *really* needed the chamber pot now.

In the end, it didn't matter. There was no time to tell Fred anything, because Odolf had already taken matters into his own hands and was charging into the cave like a hero... the sort of hero who waited until the danger had passed and *then* charged in to save the day. Which wasn't a bad kind of hero to be, all things considered. Maybe his recent brushes with giant fish and vicious soldiers and all-round-mean-and-nasty necromancers had taught him to be a bit less impulsive and headstrong when it came to dangerous situations. Emba was glad to see he hadn't lost his heroic streak entirely though. It was still brave of Odolf to go charging in first, ahead of them.

Chapter 2
The Cave of Catastrophic Chaos

Emba left the safety of her hiding place and hurried towards the cave after Odolf. But then something caught her eye, stopping her in her tracks. She forgot all about her bladder as she stood outside the entrance, gazing up at the misty ghost-dragon curled up on the rocky overhang like a cat. An enormous cat with a long, spiked tail and scales the size of dinner plates. Oh yes, and wings. Not much like a cat after all then, but as the dragon reached down one of its powerful front legs, stretching out a ghostly, glistening claw towards Emba, she wanted to stroke it all the same. Or at least touch it.

"Mum?" Emba asked, as she reached out her fingers towards the gleaming claw. The word felt strange and clumsy in her mouth. Fred had been all the family Emba had ever known, all the family she'd ever needed—until now. But when the dragon had first appeared at the cave a week before and Emba had learnt the true story of her birth—of her *hatching*—it had awakened strange new fears and yearnings inside her. "Mum," she said again. "Is that you?"

The dragon let out a low, moaning noise that might have meant anything from 'yes', to 'no' to 'look at the state of you—when was the last time you brushed your hair?'. But as Emba's hand reached through the misty sheen of the creature's enormous talon and out the other side, a tingling rush of warmth came coursing up her arm towards her heart. That was all the answer she needed. And that was all the answer she was getting. The dragon blinked its enormous milky eyes—once, twice, three times—and drew back its claw.

The air around the cave seemed to tremble as it reared up onto its colossal hind legs and let out a roar. An ear-splitting *rooooaaaaggghhhrrrr* that would have made the hairs on the back of Emba's neck stand up if she had any. The only hairs Emba had were the ones on her head. She *did* have scales though—thick lizard-like scales on her arms and legs that seemed to have spread up to her shoulders over the last few days—and *they* were prickling at the sound of the dragon's roar. But then, as the dragon stretched out its huge, boned wings and took to the sky, the roar became a rush of wind behind it. All Emba could hear now was the rhythmic swish of its wings, beating against the air like a warning: *Beware. Beware. Beware.*

Emba watched as the dragon circled up towards the red crack in the sky.

Beware. Beware. Be...

And then it was gone, leaving a strange, hollow feeling inside her chest.

Emba thought of all the things she hadn't said as she stared wistfully after the retreating dragon. *Thank you for watching over me, for coming to warn me. Thank you for rescuing my egg from Necromalcolm and bringing it here to safety after his spell went wrong. I know what he did to make that spell now. I know how he caught you and stole your blood by force, adding it to his cauldron along with his own blood. He might be my father, but I'm glad he failed. I'm glad you escaped. And even though I'm not ready for these changes that keep happening to me—the dragon eyes, the dragon scales, the dragon's blaze—I* am *glad I finally got to meet you.*

"Mum," Emba murmured again, as the red crack in the sky faded. It wasn't a question this time though. It was a hundred half-formed thoughts and unspoken feelings all rolled into a single word. But then Fred, who must have waddled straight past while Emba's eyes were fixed on the sky, let out a loud cry of alarm and Emba shook herself back to more earthly concerns. To thoughts of strangers in her home and the tight, squeezy feeling in her bladder.

She hurried on into the cave after her guardian, relieved to find the old lady safe and well after her fearful cry. But that was as far as Emba's relief went. She could have wept when she saw what had happened to their nice, cosy home. Emba stood there in shock, staring around at the wreckage. Everywhere she looked she saw chaos and destruction. Clay beakers lay in splinters on the floor beside boot-trampled herbs and smashed pots of flour. Her heavy winter cloak—a precious gift from the cloth merchant whom Fred had helped the year before—lay in sword-slashed shreds on the floor. Even Fred's stool, which Emba and Odolf had painstakingly carved for her the previous winter, lay upturned and broken-legged in the cold ashes of the fire.

An icy trickle ran down Emba's spine. It was nothing to do with the dripping stalactite above her head though. This was a trickle of fear.

"I've checked your bedroom," announced Odolf, his pale face emerging through the narrow crawl hole that separated Emba and Fred's sleeping space from the rest of the cave. "Whoever was here, they've definitely gone."

"What about the Tome?" asked Fred, her voice hoarse and husky with worry, and her left eye on twitching overdrive. She hobbled over to the concealed stone recess at the back of the cave and tugged aside the slashed wall hanging. "Oh, thank goodness," she gasped, pulling out the ancient Tome of Terrible

Tomorrows and clutching it to her chest like a baby. A very heavy, dusty baby. "They didn't find it." Fred blew away the layer of white dust that always clung to the Tome's cover no matter how recently it had been used, and tucked it tenderly back into its stone alcove.

"They probably weren't looking for it then," said Emba. Whoever 'they' were, they'd done a pretty thorough job of searching the cave. If they'd wanted to steal the Tome of Terrible Tomorrows, it would be long gone by now. But Fred and Emba didn't have anything else worth stealing. And if they weren't there for the Tome, then…

Emba's hand moved instinctively to the leather pouch she wore around her neck, as another icy trickle of fear wriggled its way down her spine. The pouch was a protective charm, filled with shards of Fred's super-long, super-powerful toenails, to keep Necromalcolm from seeing Emba in his scrying bowl. But would toenails be enough to protect her now? "They were looking for us," she said out loud. "I saw the dragon again when we got back too. I think she was trying to warn me that we're still in danger now, even though they've gone."

"The dragon?" repeated Odolf. "You mean it's here? I wish *I* could see it."

"No," said Emba. "She's gone again now, just like whoever did *this*." She pointed to the smashed beakers and Fred's broken stool. "They must have been angry when they didn't find anyone here. That's why they destroyed everything. Out of frustration, or as a warning." It was the only explanation that made any sense. "Necromalcolm must have sent them," she added, her voice turning quivery at the edges. "He must have escaped out of the cauldron like you said, Odolf. That lizard you spotted—it *must* have been him. And he's been building up his magic again these last few days, regaining his strength and getting ready to strike... And now he's sent out his henchmen to find me... to drag me back to his horrible tower... to the cauldron... and... and..."

"Hush now," said Fred, as Emba collapsed, sobbing in her arms. "You're safe with us. We won't let anything happen to you, will we Odolf?"

But it was a hollow promise and Emba knew it.

She'd seen Necromalcolm's powers first-hand. She'd seen the dark spirits he summoned to do his bidding, and the cruel hunger in his eyes. A hunger for her blood. And she knew he wouldn't stop until he'd got what he wanted.

"We don't even know for sure that he *did* escape," Fred said, stroking Emba's hair. "Maybe it really *was* just a lizard Odolf saw."

"It was quite an evil-looking wizard, now I think about it," said Odolf. "I mean, *lizard*," he corrected himself. Fred shot him a look—a 'keep-quiet-you're-not-helping' sort of look. But Odolf took no notice. "There was something about his eyes," he went on, "and the way he flicked his tail at me as he scuttled off into the shadows. Yes, the more I think about it, the more I think it *was* Necromalcolm. But I know how we can find out for sure."

"How?" asked Emba. She didn't know what Odolf was planning but she was pretty sure she wouldn't like it.

"The scrying bowl."

Odolf had insisted on bringing Necromalcolm's

scrying bowl back with them from the tower, along with his jewelled blood-collecting goblet, but the very thought of it made Emba feel queasy. It was the scrying bowl that had led Necromalcolm to her in the first place.

"No," she said firmly. "We don't even know how to use it."

"Yes, we do," said Odolf. "You fill it with water and stare into it and it shows you what—or who—you want to see. We can ask it to show us Necromalcolm. If there's nothing *to* see, then we know we're safe. And if it shows us an evil-looking lizard then we know we're not. Although, until he finds a way to return to his human form, he can't do too much harm. Can he?"

Emba wasn't so sure about that, judging by the state of the cave.

"No," she said again. "It's *his* bowl. It probably wouldn't work for us anyway."

Odolf wasn't giving up yet though. "I bet it would work for you. You're his daughter after all. It's his blood flowing through your veins."

"No, no, *no!*" Emba felt a sudden rush of fiery

heat inside her chest. Her dragon's blaze. It took every single ounce of self-control she had to keep the flames from bursting out of her mouth. She took a deep, cooling breath and swallowed. Hard. "No," she said again, more softly, as a single plume of smoke escaped from her lips. "I don't want to have anything to do with his magic." What if it wasn't only her father's blood she shared? What if she'd inherited his darkness too? Maybe it was lurking inside of her, even now, waiting to be unlocked...

"It's alright, Emba dear. You don't have to do anything you don't want to," said Fred. "We'll do what we always do and consult the Tome of Terrible Tomorrows. It won't be able to tell us what's already happened—it only deals with the future, as you know—but it might tell us if we're still in danger from Necromalcolm." She paused for a moment, as if she was thinking something through. "Not here though. It's not safe. If whoever did this *was* looking for you, who's to say they won't come back?"

"We can go to my place," said Odolf. "They'll never find you there."

Chapter 3

The Tome of Predictably Terrible Tomorrows

The Tome was as dusty as ever when Fred fetched it out of its hidden stone alcove a second time. She blew away the fresh layer of white dust from the front cover to reveal the eight-legged sea monster design waiting underneath and passed the book to Emba to carry. But Emba passed it straight on to Odolf and went to retrieve her spare goatskin bag from the bedroom (her regular bag having been confiscated at the castle), along with her second-best scaring-off-stone. If they *were* still in danger, she needed to be ready.

"Ooof," Odolf grumbled as he led the way back out of the cave and into the woods. "This thing weighs a tonne."

"That's the weight of all our futures you've got

there," said Fred, hobbling along behind him. "You be careful with it."

Odolf's treetop shelter was completely hidden from sight at ground level. A casual stroller ambling through Witchingford Woods could pass right underneath his carefully constructed sleeping platform without knowing. Unless it was night-time of course, and Odolf was snoring. But even then, if the passer-by were to look up with their lantern for the source of the terrible, pig-like snorting, there'd be nothing to see but branches and leaves.

Locating Odolf's shelter was hard enough. Actually *reaching* it, up the knotted rope ladder he kept tucked away inside a hollow trunk, was even harder. Odolf didn't usually bother with the ladder—he had his own route up and down, clambering through the branches—but Fred's tree-climbing days were well and truly behind her now. It took a considerable amount of grunting and groaning, of underarm tugging from above and under-bum pushing from below, to get her up—but at last she was there.

Odolf laid the Tome of Terrible Tomorrows down

on the old barrel top that served as a table, and Fred got straight to work.

"*I call on you, oh Ancient Tome,*" she chanted, still a little breathless from her climb.

"*To show me what will be,*
Those Terrible Tomorrows
That await inside of thee.
Reveal to me the dreaded course
The cruel Fates have decreed
For she who stands before you now,
Your supplicant in need."

No sooner were the words out of Fred's mouth than her body grew rigid and her eyes rolled up inside their sockets. Her mouth dropped open and her head began to rock backwards and forwards, faster and faster, as the Powers of Dreadful Divination took hold. And then came the dribbling—a thin line of drool oozing from her open lips into the white prickle of her chin whiskers, as her fingers flicked through the gold-edged pages of the Tome, waiting for the right prophecy to reveal itself.

Any second now, thought Emba. *Any second n—*

There! Fred let out a loud shuddering gasp, snatching her fingers away from the Tome as if they'd been stung. Her eyes rolled back into position and her face and body returned to normal.

"What is it?" asked Emba, too impatient to wait. "What does it say?"

"Is it the Final Prophecy?" asked Odolf, peering over the old woman's shoulder. "Has the time come? What about my belt buckle? Does it say anything about that?"

"Hush now, both of you," said Fred. "Give me a chance to read it."

Emba held her breath, willing her guardian to hurry up and tell her if Necromalcolm was back or not.

"*Evil stirs*," Fred began, with a slight quiver in her voice, "*beneath the scales,*

As sleeping forces wake,
As fleshless bones begin to glow
And stony mountains shake.
A treasure lost ere long is found
By one who heeds the call
Of secrets under stony spines

Within the hidden hall."

"A treasure lost," cried Odolf. "It must mean my buckle! Wait a minute, what does 'ere long' mean?"

"Before long," said Fred.

Emba could have told him that. But she was too busy worrying about the first line of the prophecy to concern herself with the treasure part. *Evil stirs beneath the scales.* Odolf must have been right about the lizard after all then. Unless... Unless it meant *her* scales. What if evil was stirring inside of *her*? What if meeting her father had awakened something in her blood? No, she'd be able to tell. Wouldn't she?

"And where do you think the hidden hall is?" asked Odolf. "What does stony spines mean?"

Fred laid a gnarled hand on his arm. "Shh, be quiet for a bit, Odolf. Let me think... No," she said at last. "I don't think the prophecy's referring to your belt buckle. That's not what it means."

Odolf didn't look convinced. "So what *is* the lost treasure then?"

"I'm not sure," said Fred. "But I think I know *where* it is. 'Stony spines' sounds like the Petrified Peaks—a series of spiked ridges on one of the mountains in the Ruinous Rockies. From a certain angle they look like a sleeping spike-backed dragon who's been turned to stone. According to legend, there's a hidden crypt underneath the base of the mountain, but no one's ever found the way in."

"But if the thieves who stole my belt buckle had discovered the secret entrance," said Odolf, "it would be the *perfect* place to store all their stolen loot. Including my buckle. Why else would the Tome of Terrible Tomorrows be telling us to go there? Necromalcolm must be back—that's what that bit about the evil under the scales means, doesn't it? And the sleeping force of his magic will be waking up again as soon as he finds a way to regain his human form." Odolf nodded to himself, looking pleased with his powers of interpretation. "And if we want to stop him, we're going to need that belt buckle. How far away are the Petrified Peaks?"

"Too far to go rushing off without a proper plan," said Fred firmly. "Especially not in the dark. Then again, I'm not sure it's safe for us to stay at the cave either."

"Perhaps we could stay here, with Odolf, tonight," suggested Emba. "And leave first thing tomorrow… unless it's *my* scales the evil is stirring beneath. What if *I'm* the one you need protecting from?"

Fred took Emba in her arms and held her tight. "You don't have an evil bone in your body. You're nothing like your father and you never will be."

Emba breathed in the old lady's words, along with her comforting musty-herb scent, hoping she was right.

Chapter 4

The Wanted Waifs of Witchingford Wood

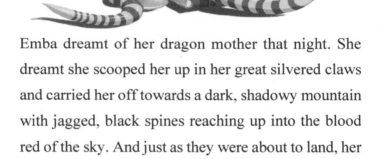

Emba dreamt of her dragon mother that night. She dreamt she scooped her up in her great silvered claws and carried her off towards a dark, shadowy mountain with jagged, black spines reaching up into the blood red of the sky. And just as they were about to land, her mother cried out to her, shaking her roughly by the leg and telling her to wake up…

Wait a minute, that wasn't a dragon cry; it was an *Odolf* cry. And those felt more like human hands than dragon claws. Emba blinked herself out of sleep to find Odolf staring down at her with an anguished look on his face.

"Wake up, Emba. Hurry," he said.

For a moment, she was confused by the brightness

of the light shining in through the cave, and then she remembered she wasn't *in* the cave. She was lying on the hard, wooden sleeping platform of Odolf's treetop shelter, with her scaring-off stone clutched tight in her fingers.

"What time is it?" Emba asked groggily. "What's happening?" And then, as the first wave of panic hit her, "Where's Fred?"

A loud snore from behind was all the answer she needed on that score though.

"It's morning," said Odolf, "and we need to go. *Now.*" He turned his attention to Fred, tapping her on the shoulder. "Wake up. We need to go," he said again.

His efforts were met with a snort followed by a soft groan. "Ooh, ow, my poor aching bones," said Fred, as Emba helped her up into a sitting position. "I'm not sure this sleeping platform agrees with me. Now then, Odolf. What was that you were saying?"

Odolf took a deep breath. "I was awake really early—thanks to someone snoring right in my ear—so I took Necromalcolm's goblet down to the market to trade in for some supplies. For our journey," he added.

"For food and drink and some warmer clothes."

Good idea, thought Emba, remembering how hungry she'd been on the long trek to Gravethorn Castle the week before. So hungry she'd resorted to eating a raw turnip, and a *rotten* raw turnip at that.

"And I found this," said Odolf, retrieving a scroll of paper from his tunic and unrolling it. "Look." It was a 'Wanted' notice, offering a hefty reward from the duchess of Gravethorn for information regarding the whereabouts of a pair of criminals… A rather young pair of criminals, judging by the pictures drawn underneath: a girl with long, knotty hair and a scrawny-looking boy with only one eyebrow.

Emba gasped. "But that's…"

"Yes," said Odolf. "That's us." His voice grew louder and wilder. "Which means it's not just whoever was in the cave last night who's looking for us now. It's *everyone*."

"Hush now," said Fred, leaping into action. It was more of a slow creak into action, truth be told, requiring the support of both Emba and Odolf to pull her up onto her feet. But once she was finally vertical, the old lady took charge of the situation with impressive decisiveness. "Right," she said. "Good work on spotting that notice, Odolf. Did you happen to see it before or after you'd got the supplies for our journey?"

"The supplies!" cried Odolf. "I was in such a rush to come back and warn you, I clean forgot about them!" He reached back into his tunic and pulled out the jewelled blood-collecting goblet. The mere sight of it sent a flutter of panic through Emba's body.

"Never mind," said Fred. "We'll have to manage without them for now. You did the right thing, coming straight back to warn us, Odolf," she added to reassure him. "Well done." She thought for a moment. "We'll head for Hibbert's Hill. It's more or less on our way and I've got an old friend there who'll be able to help us with shelter and provisions. And if we leave now, we should have a good start on anyone who's looking for us. As long as we keep away from the roads and open ground, we'll be fine. Odolf, you bring the Tome, and Emba..."

"Yes?" Emba awaited her instructions.

"You can empty the chamber pot and help me back

down that ladder."

Great, Emba thought. *Odolf's in charge of the entire future fate of the world, and I'm in charge of the toilet.* But she did as she was asked, without complaint. She didn't complain when she tripped over a hidden tree root and sent the contents of the chamber pot splashing everywhere. She didn't even complain when Fred misjudged her step coming down from the tree and caught her in the face with one of her long, gnarled toenails. *Ouch!* It didn't matter how magic her guardian's toenails were, they were still painfully sharp (and disgusting), but Emba kept her discomfort to herself and concentrated on the task in hand. The sooner they were out of there, the better.

"So, who is this friend of yours?" Odolf asked Fred as they trudged along at a painfully sluggish pace. Perhaps it was a good job he hadn't managed to fetch fresh supplies for the journey, Emba decided. They'd have struggled to carry them along with Emba's bag,

Necromalcolm's goblet and scrying bowl, the Tome of Terrible Tomorrows *and* Odolf's wooden spear. Odolf paused to readjust his grip on the Tome, before carrying on with his questioning. "Are you sure we can trust him?"

Emba had been wondering the same. In all the years she'd known Fred—her entire lifetime—the old woman had never once mentioned a friend at Hibbert's Hill. Not that Emba could remember, anyway. She couldn't recall a single visit to or from anyone at that address. In fact, she was pretty sure she'd never even *heard* of Hibbert's Hill before today.

"His name's Howard," said Fred. "But locals know him better as the Hushed Hermit of Hibbert's Hill. And I can guarantee that he won't tell *anyone* where to find us. Not a soul."

"How can you be so sure?" asked Emba.

"Because he's a hermit, like me," said Fred, as if the answer was obvious, "with no interest in worldly wealth. A reward means nothing to a man like Howard." She chuckled to herself. "And besides, he took a vow of silence thirty years ago and he's not broken it yet."

Emba was both pleased, and a little worried, to hear this. "When you say *no* interest in worldly wealth, that doesn't mean he lives on air and water, does it?" Last night's cold dinner of foraged jackabay nuts and a few measly berries—squashed berries at that—had done little to curb her homecoming hunger, and she'd been hoping that the 'provisions' on offer would be something more substantial.

Fred chuckled again. "Howard likes his air and water as much as the next man, but if I remember correctly, he's also rather partial to squirrel fritters and wild parsley mash. With gooseberry crumble for afters."

Mmm, squirrel fritters… Emba's stomach growled in anticipation.

"Really, Emba dear, you mustn't worry," Fred continued. "Howard will look after us. We'll be perfectly warm and well-fed. Not to mention comfortable. Did I mention he makes his own duck-down pillows and weaves his own blankets?"

No, Fred hadn't mentioned that, but Emba liked the sound of it. "And how long will it take to get there?"

Lunchtime would be good. In time for a late breakfast would be even better.

Fred's face fell. "At this rate of progress, I'd say we should be there sometime tomorrow morning."

"So where are we going to sleep tonight?" Emba didn't even try to keep the disappointment out of her voice. The thought of another full day's walking on an empty stomach was almost too much to bear. But heading back to the cave and being turned over to the duchess's guards wasn't much of an alternative. The duchess might be the one who'd put up the reward money, but it was her brother, Necromalcolm, who was really behind the wanted notice. Emba was sure of it. He was the one who was so keen on finding them again.

Fred thought for a moment. "With a bit of luck we might make it to the Stone Circle of Certain Doom by nightfall," she said.

Emba didn't like the sound of that. "And if we're *not* lucky enough to get that far?"

"Then we're in trouble," said Fred. "Because if we're not safely through the Screeching Swamp of Slimebane Hollow by the time it gets dark, we're sunk. Literally."

"We're already in trouble," hissed Odolf. "Did you hear that? It sounds like soldiers!"

"Quick, get in!" said Fred, pointing to a particularly spiky-looking patch of shrubs. "We won't be able to outrun them but perhaps we can give them the slip."

Odolf raised his single eyebrow. "You want us to hide in *there?* We'll be torn to pieces."

"I'll go first and hold the branches out of the way for you," Emba offered. The thought of being ripped to shreds by vicious three-inch spikes didn't exactly fill her with enthusiasm, but neither did getting caught by the duchess's guards. "My scales should give me *some* protection," she added, swallowing a yelp as the first vicious spike embedded itself deep in her hand.

"No," said Fred. "That's no way to treat a prickly-pinch shrub. You have to tickle it into submission. Here, I'll show you." She leant forwards and tickled the underside of one of the leaves. The shrub shivered and shook, letting out a high-pitched giggle as its spikes retracted back into the woody stems.

Fred pushed on into the heart of the shrub, tickling

as she went.

"Wow!" gasped Emba. "That's amazing!"

"Less gawping, more tickling," replied Fred's disembodied voice from deep inside the shrubbery.

Emba and Odolf followed suit, tickling as they pushed deep into the undergrowth towards a small, natural hollow in the middle where Fred was waiting for them.

"That's enough," she whispered. "Stop tickling and stay quiet."

The spikes had barely pushed themselves back out to their flesh-tearing fullness when the sound of soldier's voices came drifting towards the hidden trio.

"What about down that path there?" called a low, rasping voice. "Any sign of them?"

Emba held her breath. *Please don't let them find us.*

"Nah," came a slightly less rasping reply. "Nothing down this way. Just some bushes. Nasty ones with big old spikes."

"Nothing this way either," came a third voice. "I say we try down by the river."

"Good idea. Here, do you reckon *we'll* get a reward

from the duchess if we find them?"

"If by 'reward' you mean not getting our heads chopped off for *not* finding them, then yes," answered the first soldier.

"Phew," said Odolf, as the voices died away again. "That was a close one."

"A little too close," agreed Fred. "That's why we need to get to the Screeching Swamp. It would take a very brave and foolish band of soldiers to follow us across *there*."

Chapter 5

The Screeching Swamp
of Slimebane Hollow

After a long day's trudging, hiding and shrub-tickling, a deadly, vicious swamp was the last place the weary travellers wanted to be. But that's where they found themselves, and that's exactly where they'd stay, according to Fred, if they didn't make it across in time.

The Screeching Swamp more than lived up to its name, although it wasn't the swamp itself that was doing the screeching: it was its would-be victims. Odolf let out a high-pitched squeal of terror every time his foot disappeared into the oozing, green mud (which was pretty much every step), while Emba's throat was sore from screeching before they were even halfway across. It felt like invisible hands, reaching up through the slurping ground to drag her down to the murky depths. Like a living creature—a giant, hundred-handed mud monster intent on swallowing her whole.

"Hush," Fred told them for the thirteenth time in as many minutes. "The swamp feeds on fear, remember. The more you scream, the further down you'll sink. As long as you keep away from the blood-coloured patches and think nice, cheery thoughts, you'll be fine."

But it was hard to think nice, cheery thoughts on an empty stomach, with slimy swamp hands reaching up through the green ooze to grab at their ankles. As for what unseen horrors might be lurking underneath the blood-coloured patches, they were enough to make *anyone* scared. The sight of the sun dropping lower and lower in the sky wasn't doing much for Emba's peace of mind either. She racked her brain trying to think of something nice to distract herself with. *Kittens… spring flowers… hot soup on a cold day…* but then another invisible hand reached up through the swamp for her foot and she was back to screaming.

"You're doing really well," said Fred. That was a lie and Emba knew it. They *all* knew it. Any minute now the sun was going to disappear behind the hills and they wouldn't be able to pick out the dangerous, green mud from the absolutely lethal drown-if-you-step-on-it red mud. "How about a song?" Fred suggested. "Something nice and cheerful to lift our spirits and see us through to the other side." She didn't wait for an answer, clearing her throat and starting off on one of her old favourites, her tuneless, warbling voice carrying across the bog on the darkening evening air:

"There once was a lassie with hair like flame,

Arabella Blood was the young girl's name.

She caught the eye of a passing beast—

a fiend in search of a tasty feast.

Arabella screamed as he stretched his jaws…"

"Stop!" cried Emba, who'd heard enough. She knew what came next and it wasn't nice. "I don't think that's helping." It was hard to think of something that *would* help though. Her mind had been full of nothing but fears lately. Fears about the duchess tracking them down. Fears about Necromalcolm coming back for her blood. Fears about a grisly, mud-choked end at the bottom of the Screeching Swamp of Slimebane Hollow.

No, Emba told herself firmly, as another invisible hand reached up and clawed at her ankle. *Don't think about drowning under the mud. Think about soaring above it.* She imagined herself with dragon wings... imagined the glorious stretch of them unfurled across the sky... the steady beating flap of leathered skin between her bones as she greeted the gusting wind head on, driving up and away... *Ah, yes.* That was better. There was nothing to drag her down now. She was weightless. Carefree and light, drifting away from her earthly worries like a bird on the breeze. Soft currents of air brushed at her face as she left her old life behind her, as the earth spread itself out below her like a patchwork quilt. She could imagine it all so clearly.

It was working. Emba found herself racing ahead of the others, bounding across the swamp like a light-footed gazelle. A light-footed gazelle with smelly-swamp toes and the beat of imaginary wings echoing in her ears: *Goodbye... goodbye... goodbye...* Before she knew it, she was almost at the other side. Emba could see the solid line of grass and trees up ahead. But then she turned round to see the others and her heart sank, along with her feet. Fred was making her way slowly, but surely, to safety. Odolf was in trouble though. Serious trouble. The mud was up to his knees now and he was sinking fast, clutching on to his wooden spear for dear life, his face frozen in a wide-mouthed screech of fear.

"Think about something nice!" Emba yelled, battling to make herself heard over the sound of his screaming. "Think about..." She racked her brains. Dragon wings would be no good for Odolf. He was probably as scared of dragons as he was of drowning in the swamp. "Think about your belt buckle," she shouted. "Think about your buckle waiting for you under the Petrified Peaks. Think about threading it onto your belt and feeling the magic seeping back into your veins, making you fearless." She'd no idea *how* Odolf felt when he was wearing his buckle, or whether he really would find it waiting for him at their journey's end, but it seemed to be working. Yes, even as she watched, his left leg broke free of the mud and he staggered forwards, his right leg following with a resounding pop. And the fact that she could *hear* the pop meant that he must have stopped screaming too.

"That's it," Emba yelled over her shoulder as she freed herself again, bounding the last few yards to safety. "Come on, Odolf Bravebuckle, you can do this!"

She collapsed onto the grass in a panting heap, revelling in the solid hardness of the ground beneath her. For a moment there, she really *had* wished for dragon wings to carry her away, but only for a moment. This was where she belonged, with her beloved guardian Fred and her dear friend Odolf, both of whom were only a short distance from safety now. A few more steps and... yes, they'd done it! And without a second to spare. No sooner were the three of them reunited, Fred clasping the children to her chest in the full fierceness of a mother's hug, than the sun dropped below the horizon, turning the greens and reds of the swamp a dim, murky grey.

"Phew! Well done," said Fred. "That was good thinking about the belt buckle, Emba."

"Yes," agreed Odolf. "I focused on using it to protect us all from Necromalcolm, once I get it back, and that stopped me from sinking. How about you?" he asked, turning to Emba. "You must have been thinking of something amazing, given how fast you whipped across that last stretch."

Emba was glad of the darkness to hide her blushes. "Freshly baked scones," she fibbed. She could hardly admit that she'd been fantasising about flying away and leaving them both. "Tell us about this stone circle of certain doom you're taking us to, Fred," she said, changing the subject. "What does the 'certain doom' part mean, exactly?"

"It means we might have escaped from the swamp but we're still going to die," joked Odolf. At least Emba *hoped* it was a joke.

"Nonsense," said Fred. "We'll be perfectly safe there, I prom—" She stopped short, the second half of the word 'promise' dying on her lips. "We'll be fine," she corrected herself. "They're stories, that's all. Come on, we're nearly there now. If my memory serves me right, it's just the other side of those trees."

"What *sort* of stories?" asked Emba as they set off through the dusk towards the dark hill up ahead.

"Some people say the stones are a protective circle to guard whoever seeks sanctuary within them," said Fred.

Emba let out a small sigh of relief. *Oh!* That didn't sound so bad! Quite the opposite in fact.

But Fred hadn't finished yet. "And others believe that it's a dreadful, cursed spot and the stones are evil witches who resume their flesh-and-blood form by the light of a full moon, to wreak their terrible revenge on humankind."

Ah yes, that sounded worse. Much worse. Emba had never been very fond of cursed spots, or curses in general come to that, and the thought of evil witches chilled her to her bones. She'd listened to enough wild, witchy stories round the fire to know that even regular witches were bad news, let alone evil ones.

"But that's what makes it the perfect place for us to bed down for the night," said Fred. "With a bit of luck, the curse legend will keep everyone else away, including any passing soldier search parties."

"I suppose so," Emba agreed, hoping she was right. But her first glimpse of the Stone Circle of Certain

Doom, standing pale and ghostly in the gloom, did little to set her mind at ease. No wonder people thought there was a curse on the place.

Up close, the stone circle was creepy—very creepy—but it *was* still a stone circle, Emba was relieved to discover. Not a cackling witch circle. Not yet anyway. It was easy enough to see how the story had come about though. Easy enough to imagine that the towering stones' peculiar lumps and bumps were really petrified noses and chins, and evil pointing fingers. She shivered in the cold air, wishing Odolf had remembered the supplies after all. She could have done with some warmer clothes and blankets. And food. Yes, food would have been good too. And maybe something to keep witches away, just in case…

Odolf seemed nervous as well. Emba could hear him muttering under his breath: "It's only a story. Only a story." But until recently, Emba had thought *dragons* only existed in stories. And if dragon stories were true, who was to say that stories of stone-turned witches weren't true too?

She found herself thinking about Necromalcolm

again as she glanced from one witch-like stone to another. About the shocking moment where he'd lifted up his long necromancer's robe to reveal tree trunk legs, with roots instead of feet, reaching down into the stone floor beneath him and anchoring him to the spot. If someone as powerful and evil as him could be held in place by magic, maybe witches could too—ready to turn back into their living forms once the moonlight was bright enough to break the spell.

Emba clutched at her leather pouch of toenail shards. Where *was* the moon anyway? Was it full enough to set them free? She turned her gaze upwards, wondering which of the invisible clouds it might be hiding behind. But even as she stood there searching the sky, the clouds shifted and the moon appeared big and bright and round, like a great white eye looking down on the stone circle below. At the *witch* circle below. Emba froze in horror as a cold, claw-like hand reached out from behind and grabbed her.

Chapter 6

The Stone Circle of Certain Doom

Emba didn't know whether to scream for help or plead for mercy. Whether to reach for her scaring-off stone or run, but her brain was as frozen as her legs. As the witch's fingers tightened round her arm, Emba felt like *she'd* been turned to stone too. Her nose was still working though, the rancid smell of sulphur and rotten flesh filling her nostrils.

"Please," she squeaked. *Please don't lock me up or turn me into an animal or…*

"Dinner time," rasped the witch, her breath warm and wet against the back of Emba's neck.

No, no, no. "Please," Emba squeaked again as a wild trembling took hold of her body. "Please don't eat me."

"Eat you?" The witch chuckled to herself. A Fred-sounding sort of chuckle. "To be honest, I was thinking of something a little less chewy," she said. "Toasted mushrooms, maybe."

"Oh," Emba breathed. "It's you!" She twisted her head round to see Fred holding up a pair of giant blue stench caps—mushrooms so disgustingly stinky that most people wore pegs on their noses to harvest them. "I thought..."

Fred chuckled again. "You thought I was a wicked old hag come to boil you up in a cauldron and suck the meat off your bones? Charming."

"Of course not," Emba fibbed, feeling silly. "It's this place. It gives me the creeps." That was putting it mildly. The thought of the wicked, stone-trapped crones leering down at her gave Emba the full-on terrors. And that was *before* anyone had mentioned boiling cauldrons. If there was one thing Emba Oak hated, after her recent adventures, it was cauldrons. And lizards. And screeching swamps. And stone witches. And the smell of blue stench caps wafting under her nostrils. A gagging sound caught in her throat as she made the mistake of breathing in through her nose. "*Ugghhkkk.* Get those mushrooms away from my face," she begged. "Please."

Fred smiled at her through the gloom. "It'll be better once we've got a nice fire going," the old lady promised, "you'll see."

Mmm, fire, Emba thought. *Beautiful, burning tongues of flame. Yes, fire would make everything better.* She drifted away for a second, her mind filled with hot, orange sparks and cracklings.

"And the mushrooms will be fine when they're cooked," Fred added, brandishing them in the air as she spoke and sending fresh waves of nauseating foulness straight up Emba's nose. The smell brought her back to her senses with a lurch. Back to the moonlit stone circle and the prickling feelings of fear under her skin. Emba shook her head, as if to shake away any last stray thoughts of fire. Was it her dragon blood that had her dreaming of flickering flames again? Or was it just a sign of how cold she was?

"Why don't you and Odolf see if you can find some firewood, while I sniff out a few more blue stench caps for dinner?" said Fred.

Firewood. Yes. Hot blazing fire… And just like that the flames were back again, filling Emba with the same strange longing. She could almost feel the fire radiating out of her, lighting up the dark stone circle like the sun. It was so bright she could pick out every little detail and colour clearly now—from the white eye-like splashes of bird poo glaring out of the rock on the far side of the circle, to the mossy green warts adorning its stony skin. But Emba didn't stop to think about how, or why she could see so well all of a sudden. She was more focused on the dancing flames in her mind than her new powers of sight. *Beautiful, burning fire…*

Somewhere, beyond the crackle and hiss in her head, she could still hear Fred talking though: "We need to keep our strength up if we're going to make it all the way to Hibbert's…" But then the old lady broke off with a gasp. "Emba," she cried. "Your eyes!"

What? Emba dragged herself back to reality. *Oh no,* she thought, *it's happening again, isn't it?* Her eyes must be glowing, the black pupils changing from black dots to long dragon-like slits. *Dragon eyes—* that's what Necromalcolm had called them. *You've got the dragon eyes.* And after the dragon eyes had come the dragon's breath: the clouding smoke spilling from her nose and mouth. And after *that* came the dragon's blaze: the fierce rush of flame that had blasted the necromancer back into his own bubbling cauldron. What if the same thing happened again? What if Emba accidentally turned her dragon fire on Fred?

She swallowed hard, shielding her eyes with her hand as she tried to blink them back to normal. "Firewood. Yes, that's a good idea," she agreed, anxious to get away before she hurt someone. Again. "But what about you?" she asked. "What if the stones turn into witches while we're gone?"

"I've dealt with worse than a few witches," said Fred. "And I don't think they like the smell of stench caps any more than you do. One whiff of these beauties and they'll be begging *me* for mercy." She let out another chuckle, but it was a hollow, forced-sounding laugh this time. "Honestly, I'll be fine, Emba dear. It's not even a proper full moon tonight.

I'm more worried about you," she admitted. "Are you going to be alright? With your eyes, I mean?" She laid a concerned hand on Emba's arm.

"I'm fine," said Emba. "I just need to learn how to control the dragon part of me, that's all." She blinked again, thinking cooling thoughts of morning dips in the pond they used for bathing. Of icicles hanging from the cave entrance in winter. Of thick snow covering the wood like a chilly, white blanket… Yes, that was better. The world was growing darker again already, the sharpness of her vision softening as the bright light faded back to silvery moonlight.

"Come on," called Odolf, propping his trusty spear up against one of the stone witches and setting off in search of wood. "The sooner we get a fire going, the sooner I can dry out my swamp-filled boots."

Emba followed after him, searching the ground for fallen branches and sticks. And maybe, if she was lucky, some berries to take away the taste of the stench caps. It was hard work in the dark though. Where was her new dragon sight when she actually needed it? Twice she reached for a berry on a bush, only to discover it was a gorse-rat dropping. *Yuck!*

"Over here," called Odolf. "There's enough wood here for ten campfires!"

Emba peered through the gloom, trying to work out where his voice was coming from. Ah yes, there he was. She hurried over to join him, taking her paltry collection of three twigs and a horned dusk moth with her. The moth wasn't for burning, or eating, but had settled on her arm during the search and seemed in no hurry to leave.

Odolf was standing by a cluster of trees, cradling an impressive collection of branches to his chest. "These should keep us going for a while," he said. "Do you want to get some smaller bits for kindling? There are some nice dry twigs down there under that oak."

"Alright," Emba agreed, dropping into a low crouch and scooping the sticks straight up into her lap. "Will that be enough, do you think, or shall I—?" The rest of the sentence died on her tongue as something rustled in the undergrowth beside her. "What was that?" she gasped. "Look! A tail! A lizard tail!" Emba fell backwards in fright, scrambling to get away, sending the twigs spilling out of her lap onto the ground.

"Where?" asked Odolf. "I can't see anything."

Emba pointed to the long, green tail sticking out from a pile of dead leaves. The lizard was lying very still, as if it was waiting for something. As if it was plotting its next move and preparing to strike. "It's him!" she cried, her voice wild with fear. "It's Necromalcolm. He must have followed us here."

"Don't be silly," said Odolf dismissively. "Trust me, Emba, there's nothing there."

"IT'S HIM!" Emba yelled back. "HE'S COME TO TAKE MY BLOOD!" She pointed again, stabbing at the air with her finger.

Odolf dropped his collection of branches and bent down to investigate. "What? This old thing?" he asked, picking the lizard up by the tail and shaking it—shaking *him*—in Emba's face.

"AAGGHHHHHRRRR!" she screamed, putting up her hands to protect herself. "Get him away from me! Put him down!"

"Emba," laughed Odolf. "It's not Necromalcolm. You can relax."

"How do you know?" she hissed, still cowering behind her hands.

Odolf laughed harder. "Because it's not even a lizard. It's a bit of wild dagger grass. A bird must have dropped it."

Emba lowered her hands away from her face and peered more closely at the 'lizard'. He was right. It was only a blade of grass after all. A fat, tail-like blade, but grass all the same. *Thank goodness for that.*

"You should have seen your face." Odolf was crying with laughter now, tears of merriment streaming down his creased-up cheeks. "It's him!" he squealed, in a mocking impression of Emba's voice. "He's come to take my blood!"

"Stop it." Emba's relief turned to indignation. "It's not funny."

"No," agreed Odolf. "It's not funny. It's *hilarious*. Save me, Odolf," he teased. "Save me from the evil necromancer grass."

"Stop it," Emba said again, feeling a wave of anger building up inside her. The more Odolf laughed, the angrier she felt—angry at him for making fun of her, and angry at Necromalcolm for *still* terrorising her after everything that had happened.

"Don't worry, Emba, I'll protect you." Odolf pretended to wrestle with the offending bit of grass, dropping down onto the ground beside her and writhing around in a fake struggle to the death. "Help, no, it's too strong. I'm no match for its wicked grassy powers!"

"I *said* stop it!" Swirling plumes of smoke came pouring out of Emba's mouth as she spoke.

Odolf was too busy enjoying himself at her expense to notice. "NO! Not the spiky tip of slightly scratching doom," he cried. "Not the sneezing pollen of mortal destruction. Anything but that."

"STOP IT!" roared Emba a third time. *Oh no!* She could already feel the column of fire rushing up from her belly. She tried to swallow it back down again, but it was too late to stop it now. The burning inside her was too hot. Too fast. Too fierce. She swung her head to the side as the flames came tearing up out of her throat, trying to steer them away from her friend. The column of flame passed within a whisker of Odolf's shoulder, blasting straight into the waiting bushes behind him.

Odolf let out a terrified yelp, flattening himself against the ground, as a curtain of flames sprung up.

The burning heat in Emba's throat retreated again in shock, almost as quickly as it had come. "I'm so sorry," she spluttered, staring in a confused mixture of horror and satisfaction as the fire took hold, spreading up into a nearby tree and licking at the carpet of dry leaves and twigs underneath. It was terrible and beautiful all at the same time. But then her survival instinct kicked in and she dragged herself clear of the encroaching flames, and there was no misguided sense of beauty anymore. Just fear.

What have I done?

Chapter 7

The Scorching Circle of Even More Certain Doom

The fire was in full blaze now, devouring everything in its path.

"Run, Odolf!" Emba gasped, her breath catching at the burnt rawness of her throat. "Hurry!" But the flames were coming for him from all sides now, spitting and snapping as they chased closer... and closer...

Odolf seemed rooted to the spot, too terrified to move and save himself.

"Hurry!" Emba called again. "Please," she begged.

It was no good though. Fear seemed to have taken over her friend's body, rendering him as immobile as the witches back at the stone circle.

Emba tried another tack. "Come on. Odolf Bravebuckle isn't scared of a few flames, is he? Please,

Odolf, I need you." *I need you to get out of there and save yourself.*

Odolf finally shook himself out of his fear-fuelled trance, springing back to life. "Odolf Bravebuckle to the rescue," he called over the hungry crackle of burning wood, coughing and wheezing as he breathed the acrid smoke down into his lungs. He swung himself round in a circle, looking for the best way out. And there it was: a narrow corridor of clearance directly behind him—one last safe path through the growing ring of flames. But even as Odolf started towards it, a burning branch fell to the ground by his feet, cutting off his last available exit. There *was* no way out anymore.

"I'm trapped!" he screamed.

"Don't worry!" Emba screamed back at him. "I'm coming." She didn't even stop to think, racing towards the burning branch and picking it up with her bare hand—fingers tightening round the red-hot wood— and flinging it out of the way. She didn't stop to think and she didn't stop to feel. Emba Oak was too focused on saving her friend to allow for fear or pain.

"Come on!" she yelled, rushing into the circle of flames and grabbing hold of his arm. "This way."

It wasn't until the pair of them lay gasping on the grass at a safe distance from the blaze, that Emba stopped to wonder how she'd done it. Her hand didn't even seem to hurt, but there was no way she could have escaped unharmed. Was there? She glanced fearfully down at her palm, steeling herself against the sight of her injuries. But there were no terrible burns there to see. No blistered skin. Just glittering blue scales, flashing in the moonlight.

"My hand!" she cried. "Look!"

Emba was used to the scales on her arms and legs. She'd had them since she was born—since she'd hatched, rather—and they were as much a part of her now as her eyes and ears. She'd even got used to the new scales that had spread over her shoulders after she'd blown smoke at the attacking bear on the way to Gravethorn Castle. But this was something else again. There were tiny scales all over the back of her hand, and even tinier scales coating her fingers and palm. It was like looking at a snake's hand—if snakes *had* hands—or a lizard paw. Or… or a dragon paw.

Odolf took hold of her hand in his, running a ticklish finger across the centre of Emba's palm. She wasn't in the mood for laughing though. "Woah," he croaked. "That's… that's…"

Disgusting, thought Emba, finishing his sentence in her head. *Weird. Creepy. Freakish.* There was no shortage of terms to describe it. *Shocking. Repulsive. Grotesque.*

But Odolf had an altogether different word in mind. "That's amazing!" he said, his eyes shining with something that looked more like admiration than disgust.

Emba stared at him in surprise. "Really?"

"It's fantastic! It's as if your dragon blood knew you needed protection from the flames, so it gave you extra scales. That's like dragon magic, that is!"

Emba wasn't so sure. How could her blood have known what was going to happen before she did? How could blood know *anything,* come to that?

"You and your scales saved my life, Emba. They're amazing, and so are you."

But Odolf's praise made Emba feel worse, not better. *You wouldn't have needed saving if it wasn't for me and my stupid 'dragon's blaze'*, she thought. *I'm a danger, not a hero*. It wasn't scales over her hands she needed, it was a thick mask of scales over her mouth, to stop her from setting light to things in the first place.

A piercing chorus of squawks brought Emba's attention back to the flaming ring of bushes behind them. Except it wasn't a ring anymore. The flames had broken free from the circle and spread out along a line of dry gorse and heather, sending clouds of tiny, terrified flutterbeaks screeching up into the air ahead of them. Odolf wasn't the only one she'd put in danger, Emba realised with a sickening jolt. There must be entire colonies of birds, bugs and mice-like creatures whose homes were now under threat thanks to her inability to control her own fiery temper.

"I'm sorry," she whispered to the disappearing birds. "I'm sorry," she whispered to Odolf, as guilty tears trickled down her cheeks like rain. If only it *would* rain. She stared longingly up at the thick black cloud of smoke drifting into the night sky. If only it was a *real* cloud, grown dark and heavy with rain, ready to release its fire-quenching water on the flames below.

Rain, rain come to me, she chanted in her head, willing the weather to change.

Fall on land and fall on sea.
Rain from north and rain from east,
Rain on bird and rain on beast.
Rain from south and rain from west,
Cleanse the land and make us blessed.

Nothing happened. At least, nothing happened for a good minute or two, until a thick bank of cloud came scudding across the sky, blocking out the moon and thrusting them into darkness. For a moment, Emba wondered if *she'd* summoned it by the mere power of her mind, by the same dark magic that flowed through Necromalcolm's veins, but then dismissed the idea again as nonsense. *I'm nothing like my father*, she told herself firmly. *It's a coincidence, that's all. I just happened to be thinking the words as the weather changed.* And then there was no time for any more thinking, because the gathering clouds chose that precise moment to burst, sending a heavy wall of water cascading down on top of them. *Ow, ow, ow, ow, ow!* It felt like a thousand cold needles stabbing at her head and face, drenching her hair and clothes in a matter of seconds.

"Look!" cried Odolf, wiping water from his eyes. He pointed towards the bushes. "The fire's out already."

"It wasn't me." Emba shouted to make herself heard over the wild roar of the rain before he got any more ideas about her dragon magic. Or her necromancer's blood, come to that.

"What wasn't you?" Odolf shouted back.

"The rain. It wasn't me who summoned it. It's not *magic* rain."

But Odolf only seemed to hear the last two words. "What? Magic rain?" he repeated. "You mean *you* did this? That's amazing. But perhaps you can turn it off now before we catch our death of cold?" His teeth were chattering even as he said it.

"No, I said it *wasn't* me," Emba shouted back. But she shut her eyes against the relentless torrent of water and wished all the same. She didn't want to think about her father's powerful blood flowing through her veins, but she *did* want the rain to stop hammering on her skull. She wanted the curtain of water to stop running down her back, and she wanted it to stop pouring on her poor, bedraggled friend. Emba felt cold and shivery enough under her dripping clothes, even with her new scales to protect her. Odolf must have been ten times as cold with nothing but bare skin underneath his sodden shirt. *Please let it stop raining*, she wished. But the rain hammered down as hard as ever.

"It's no good," cried Odolf, as if he really had been expecting Emba to magic it away again. "It's getting heavier, if anything." He squelched back to the bushes to reclaim his charred (and decidedly soggy) collection of branches, calling for her to follow. "Let's get back to the stone circle and find Fred. Maybe she'll know somewhere warm and dry we can go."

Maybe, thought Emba, although she didn't hold out much hope. If Fred *did* know of somewhere warm and dry—and safe—to spend the night, why had she led them to a cold, stone circle of witches?

Chapter 8

The Relentless Rain of Wretchedness

"Th-there you are," stammered Fred as Emba and Odolf squelched their way back into the Stone Circle of Certain Doom. "I was s-starting to worry the rain had washed you away. I've n-never known anything like it." Her left eye was twitching and her teeth were chattering like crazy. Poor Fred. Emba hated to see her looking so cold and bedraggled.

"Th-that's because it's m-magic rain," said Odolf, through equally chattering teeth. He was shivering all over now. "Emba summoned it to put out the f-f-fire, but she doesn't know how to stop it."

Fred looked from one to the other of them in alarm. "M-magic?" she repeated. "F-fire? Oh my poor dears, are you alright?"

"No," said Emba. "That's not what happened. It wasn't me. I mean the fire was me but… It doesn't matter now," she said. "It's fine. We're both fine, aren't we?" Fred had been through enough lately. The long days of trudging—not to mention the days spent as a prisoner underneath Necromalcolm's tower—had clearly taken their toll on the old woman's health and Emba didn't want to add to her worries.

"F-f-fine," agreed Odolf, attempting to fix his shaking lips into a smile. "It'll take m-more than a b-bit of rain to defeat Odolf B-Bravebuckle."

A bit *of rain?* thought Emba. *That was putting it mildly.* She brought her hand up to her face, pushing a dripping lock of hair out of her eyes, and was amazed to feel how soft her finger scales were against her skin. It was almost as if they weren't there anymore. Wait! They *weren't* there anymore! Emba squinted at her hand, turning it over to examine both sides, but there was no mistake. Her latest new scales had disappeared again, as mysteriously as they'd arrived.

"Look," she gasped, showing Odolf. "My scales! They've gone."

"That's because the fire's been p-put out," he said. "Your dragon blood must have known you don't need them to protect you anymore. N-now you just need to get your *necromancer's* blood to take over and stop this rain, and everything will be back to normal."

Back to normal? Huh! Emba couldn't even remember what normal *was* anymore. There was certainly nothing normal about the idea of Necromalcolm's blood coursing through her veins. The very thought made her feel scared and queasy.

"I can't," she said. "I can't do magic. I don't *want* to do magic. I'm not like my father."

"Of c-course you're not, Emba dear," said Fred soothingly. "You couldn't *be* more different."

The old lady's reassurances didn't bring Emba as much comfort as they had before though. What if the rain's arrival wasn't a coincidence after all? What if there'd been something magic in the rhyme that popped into her mind just before the clouds started scudding across the sky? *Could* she have inherited some of her father's power? Maybe that was how it had begun with him too—with something as innocent as a weather spell—before success went to his head and darkness started to take over.

Odolf reached out and ran his wet fingers along the bottom of Emba's chin.

She batted his hand away. "What are you doing? Get off."

"Checking for a beard," he said with a chuckle. "You're alright though. I don't think you're turning into Necromalcolm just yet."

Emba giggled, despite herself. Despite the rain. Despite the cold and the dark and the circle of stone witches leering down at her from all sides. Fred was laughing too—a comforting cackle of a laugh that made Emba feel warmer inside, even though she was as cold and wet as ever on the outside. They were all laughing. And maybe their laughter was a kind of magic too—or maybe the clouds had simply run out of water—because the rain finally started to ease. It was less of a hammering now and more of a pattering. And then the pattering became a gentle dribble, before dying away altogether.

"You did it," said Odolf. "You made it stop."

The laughter died in Emba's throat. "No," she said firmly. "That wasn't me. *None* of it was me."

The rain might have stopped, but Emba, Odolf and Fred were a long way from being dry. They sat huddled together in the centre of the circle, staring at the useless pile of wet branches and Fred's collection of giant blue stench caps, which were as raw and stinky as ever. No one was laughing anymore.

"We'll never get a fire going now," said Odolf with a sigh. "Not unless..." He turned to Emba with a hopeful raise of his eyebrow.

"No," she said firmly. She didn't need to hear the end of the sentence to know what he was after. "I'm not using my dragon's blaze. It's too dangerous. I nearly got you killed last time."

"But that was because I made you properly angry," Odolf insisted. "What if I just made you a little bit cross. Just enough to get a gentle fire going?"

"You already *are* making me cross," said Emba. "I told you, the answer's 'no'. It's not worth the risk."

Odolf refused to give up though. "But if you *don't* help us start a fire, we might all die of cold. Surely you don't want to risk that?"

"Hush now, Odolf," said Fred. "You're not helping matters. If Emba doesn't want to use her dragon powers, then you need to respect that." She paused for a moment. "Although…"

Oh no, thought Emba. *Not you as well.* It was one thing refusing Odolf, but Fred was a different matter. Emba could already feel her resolve slipping away as she glanced at the old lady's deathly pale cheeks and blue-tinged lips. Maybe Odolf was right. Maybe carrying on without a fire *was* dangerous.

"We wouldn't want you to do anything you're not comfortable with," said Fred, soothingly, laying an icy hand on Emba's arm. "But learning to control your flames might be a good thing."

"What if I *can't* control it though?" said Emba. "What if I set light to something else by mistake?"

"There isn't anything else here *to* set light to," Odolf pointed out. "Apart from the witches, and flames can't hurt them. Not while they're in stone form anyway."

Fred let out an impatient sigh. "That's just a story," she said. "I told you." She paused again and smiled to herself. A sly kind of smile. "But if they really *were* witches, and the moon *was* full enough to break the spell after all, I bet the sight of a fire-breathing girl in their midst would be enough to scare them into keeping their stone form for the night."

"Alright," Emba agreed with a sigh. She knew when she was beaten. "I'll do it. But make sure you both stay behind me. We can't risk any more accidents. And I don't need *you* making me angry," she told Odolf, imagining herself swinging round to face him in a fiery rage. "I can do that perfectly well myself."

Odolf placed the damp branches in the middle of the circle and then he and Fred moved to a safe spot behind Emba's back. "All set," he called. "Off you go."

Emba fixed her gaze on the branches and tried to think angry thoughts. Angry, but not *too* angry. She thought about the terrible state of the cave... about the smashed pots and Fred's broken stool. But that only made her feel sad and scared. She thought about the thieves who'd stolen Odolf's dragon belt buckle on the way to Gravethorn Castle, taking his confidence along with it and causing him to abandon Emba to finish the journey on her own. But that was no good either. Emba couldn't think about that without remembering how Odolf had changed his mind and come back for her. How he'd risked his own life to save her from the bear. It became a happy, grateful memory that reminded her what a good friend he really was.

There was nothing else for it then. Emba took a deep breath and thought about Necromalcolm. She thought about how he'd kidnapped Fred in an effort to lure her to his tower. She thought about how he'd blasted Odolf back against the wall and left him for dead. Yes, that was better. She could feel a big angry ball of heat growing inside her already. Growing and growing. How dare he take his evil lust for dragon blood out on her friends? But the anger was too strong this time. Too powerful to control.

Stop! Emba told herself. *Think about something else. Think cold thoughts. Quick!* She thought about the tingling chill of the summer bathing pond and the glittering gleam of winter icicles. She thought about snow piling up in soft, white drifts outside the cave and the icy trickle of a melted snowball down her back. Yes, that was better. The ball of fire inside her was shrinking again to something smaller and easier to control.

She opened her mouth and blew, breathing out a single, steady line of flame. *Perfect*. Emba drew closer to the wet branches, guiding her flame towards them and watching the steam rise up as they began to dry. She wasn't thinking *anything* now—her mind was too focused on the flame. Angry thoughts had given way to a peaceful orange stillness, as the flame moved in and out to the steady rhythm of her own breath.

The branches were burning on their own now. Emba roused herself from her warm, orange trance to hear Odolf clapping and cheering behind her. "You did it!" he cried. "You actually did it." He let out an excited whoop. "I *knew* you could."

His praise was premature though. When Emba closed her mouth and swallowed, the flame started coming out of her nostrils instead. *No, no, no!* She could feel—could smell—the little hairs inside her nose burning. Emba put up her hand to pinch her nostrils together, hoping to pinch out the fire too, and then thought better of it. What if that diverted the flame somewhere even worse? She didn't want to end up with fire coming out of her ears, setting light to her own hair.

She opened her mouth again, panting like a dog and trying not to panic. *Cold thoughts*, Emba reminded herself, forcing her mind back to snow and icicles. *Even colder than that.* She imagined cutting a hole in the thick ice on Lost Hope Lake and leaping into the heart-stopping waters beneath. She imagined the frozen gasp of her own lungs and the blue chill of her skin. That was better. The flame was dwindling now. Dying. One last splutter of heat and then it was gone. *Thank goodness.* But the big fire at the centre of the stone circle burned on, warming Emba's damp clothes and filling her with an equally warm sense of relief. Of satisfaction.

I did it, she told herself, echoing Odolf's words. *I actually did it.*

Chapter 9

The Beckoning Bones

It wasn't *quite* like the cosy fire back home in the cave. It didn't come with snuggly goat-hair blankets and the smell of delicious food wafting round the stalactites. This fire came with scary stone faces and the stink of cooking stench caps. But it was enough to dry their clothes and lift their spirits, and keep the cold, dark night at bay. It was exactly what they needed to keep their *hunger* at bay too: Fred was right about the mushrooms tasting better than they smelt once they were cooked. A proper toasting had at least made them edible, and a belly full of bitter, smelly mushrooms was infinitely better than a belly full of nothing.

Fred let out a big, yellow-toothed yawn. "What a day.

I don't know about you two but I'm ready to turn in for the night." She patted the ground beside her, as if it was a pillow in need of fluffing. But the ground inside the witches' circle stayed as flat and hard as ever. Even the rain hadn't managed to soften it up.

"I think we should sleep in shifts," said Odolf, "with one of us keeping guard, in case of wild animals, or soldiers, or bounty hunters. Or thieves, looking to steal the Tome or the jewelled cup and scrying bowl." He glanced nervously round the stone circle. "Or witches."

Or wizard lizards, thought Emba, adding yet another threat to the list. They'd be lucky if they got *any* sleep, with so many dangers lying in wait for them.

"I'll go first," Odolf offered, taking up position with his spear. "After all, I'm the bravest, and the best at spotting things."

And the most boastful, thought Emba, with a quiet smile.

"I might not have my buckle back yet," he continued, "but I will soon. It's waiting for me under the spiny mountains just like the Tome said:

A treasure lost ere long is found

By one who heeds the call
Of secrets under stony spines
Within the hidden hall."

He nodded to himself. "Yes. It'll be there. It *has* to be... And in the meantime, I'm still Odolf Bravebuckle, hero of the Final Prophecy."

It was good to see his confidence had returned. Emba hoped for his sake that he was right. She hoped he really would find his precious dragon buckle waiting for him under the Petrified Peaks.

"What will you do if you *do* spot someone coming?" she asked. "What if it's a whole gang of bounty hunters? Or a pack of wolves? You won't try and take them on single-handedly, will you?" There was such a thing as too *much* confidence.

Odolf shook his head. "Of course not," he said. And then he broke into a grin. "I'll wake you up and let you blast them with your dragon's blaze. Even brave heroes need assistance sometimes."

Fred really must have been tired. So tired, in fact, that she'd forgotten the nightly lullaby charm she always sang to protect Emba. She was already snoring away, despite the hardness of the ground on her aching bones, but Emba's mind was still too full of whirring thoughts and worries for sleep: worries about turning into a dragon (or turning into her father, which was even worse) and worries about Necromalcolm coming back to finish what he'd started. She was worried about someone reporting their whereabouts to the duchess, in order to claim the reward. And she was worried about the stone witches resuming their flesh-and-blood forms during the night...

Emba sat up with a sigh and rubbed her eyes. She could see Odolf pacing round the circle, spear at the ready.

"Psst," she called, trying not to wake Fred. "Odolf."

He was there at her side in an instant. "What? What is it? What have you seen?"

"Nothing," said Emba. "Sorry, I didn't mean to

frighten you."

Odolf let out a snort of indignation. "Frighten me? I wasn't *frightened*. I was in a heroic state of high alert. There's a difference, you know."

Emba bit back a smile. "Of course," she said, solemnly. "I was just wondering if you could do me a favour?"

Odolf puffed out his chest. "A *brave* kind of favour?"

Emba shook her head. "No, not really," she admitted. "I was hoping for a story. A *nice* story to take my mind off things. One where nothing bad happens and the heroes get to live happily ever after."

"That doesn't sound like much of a story to me," said Odolf, "but I'll give it a go." He stopped his pacing and joined Emba by the fire. "Hmm, let's see… Once upon a time, there was a brave young warrior with only one eyebrow."

"Was his name Odolf, by any chance?" laughed Emba.

"No. His name was er… his name was Udolf. Udolf Bravebreeches, and he lived in the woods near a wise hermit's cave. I mean, the hermit was wise, not the cave."

"And what was the hermit called?" asked Emba.

"She was called Fr... Fr... Frank," said Odolf. "Yes, that's right. Frank, short for Winnifrank the Wise."

"Did anyone else live in the cave with Frank? No wait, let me guess. A girl called Amber with scales on her arms and legs."

"No," said Odolf. "She wasn't called Amber. She was called Omba. Omba Chestnut. And Omba and Udolf were the best of friends. They did everything together. They swam in the river and played hide-and-seek in the trees. They helped Fred, I mean Frank, gather herbs for her healing charms. They shared tales and jokes around the fire and ate squirrel stew and honey and quince scones..."

Emba closed her eyes as he talked, imagining herself back at the cave. She imagined the warm, flickering fire casting shadows up the rocky walls. She imagined the fragrant steam rising up from her bowl of stew like a plume of smoke... which somehow led her back to thoughts of her mother. Her dragon mother. But they were comforting thoughts this time. Emba thought of the gentle, tingling rush of warmth she'd felt when she'd reached out her hand to try and touch her mother's claw—a warmth that had spread all the way up her arm to her heart. And, as she sank into her memory of that warmth, Odolf's voice grew quieter and the image of the cave faded away to a warm, red nothing... and then the nothing became the sky as Emba found herself flying again, held warm and tight by mighty dragon claws. Heavy dragon wings beat out a new message above her head—*it's time, it's time, it's time*—as they soared off into the fiery redness of the night.

Time for what? Emba called out in her dream. But there was no answer.

It's time.

It's time.

It's time.

When she looked down she could see the same dark, shadowy mountain as before, its jagged black spines reaching up into the blood red of the sky. But the dream didn't stop there. Not this time. She felt a sudden swooping sensation in her stomach as her mother's wingbeat changed and they began their descent, diving down at an alarming speed.

We're going to crash, she thought, bracing herself for the coming impact. But at the last moment her mother eased back out of the dive and let go, depositing Emba on the ground before turning sharply and flying off into the night once more.

Emba found herself staring at a secret door hidden in the side of the mountain, which opened when she pressed her hand—her scaled hand—against the rock. She stepped inside, following a dark, winding tunnel down to an enormous hollowed-out chamber buried deep under the earth.

"Hello?" she called. "Is anyone there? I've come for..." But in her dream, Emba couldn't remember what she *had* come for. "Hello?" she called again.

The ground began to shift and shake beneath her feet as something big and white pushed its way up through the earth in front of her, like an enormous worm. Like the beak of a giant buried bird. Emba opened her mouth to scream but nothing came out. Her tongue seemed to have glued itself in place. She tried to run, but her legs wouldn't work properly either. All she could do was stand there and watch in horrified silence as the beak-worm emerged. Except it wasn't a worm or a beak. It was a bone. A colossal, curved rib bone.

The ground shook even harder as more bones came poking up through the floor to join it. There were leg bones and knuckle bones and an entire spine wiggling their way to freedom. There were foot bones and tail bones and a big, blind skull, with hollow eye sockets and a mouth of sharp yellow-white teeth. The bones were clambering over each other now, slotting themselves back into their allotted position as they reformed into a living skeleton.

Emba watched on in a mute mixture of horror and fascination as the creature took shape before her, lifting up its own skull and placing it back on the top of its neck. It looked like... yes, it looked like a dragon.

The dragon tipped its skull to one side as if it was observing her, drinking her in with its empty, black eye sockets.

"What?" she whispered, finally finding her voice again. "What do you want?"

It held up a long, hooked claw and beckoned to her, pointing to the swirling void of darkness that had opened up out of nowhere at the end of the chamber.

"No," Emba whimpered, as her body flooded with fear. She didn't know what was waiting there in the blackness, but she could feel the power emanating from it as she stood there, trembling. "No," she said again. "I don't want to go in there. Please don't make me." But the dragon took no notice, its bony, beckoning claw dragging her forwards as if she was attached to it by invisible threads.

"*NO!*" Emba screamed as she reached the swirling blackness beyond and tumbled inside.

She awoke with a start to the sound of dragon growls. Wait, no, not dragon growls—snoring *Fred* growls. Emba let out a soft sigh of relief as the fear and tension eased themselves back out of her body. *It was only a dream.* She peered through the darkness to see her guardian's rounded shape silhouetted against the dying glow of the fire. For a moment, she thought she saw Odolf too, standing tall and brave as he kept guard over them, but it turned out to be one of the witch-shaped stones.

Emba rolled over on the hard ground, shifting her legs to try and get more comfortable, and felt her eyelids closing again. *No, wake up*, said a voice in her head. *You need to stoke the fire before it goes out altogether.* But Emba was too sleepy for any fire-stoking. Too sleepy to wonder where Odolf was. Too sleepy to think anything more at all...

Chapter 10

The Stony Silence of Odolf Bravebuckle

Emba's body felt stiff all over when she woke up the next morning. Stiff and cold and aching. She must have slept right through her turn for guard duty. Why hadn't Odolf woken her?

A thick fog hung over the stone circle like a damp, white blanket, as she stared, bleary-eyed, at the dead ashes of the fire. She could have done with a *real* blanket to wrap round her frozen shoulders—like the warm woollen one the dungeon guard had confiscated the week before, to stop her getting too comfy—but Emba was out of luck on that score. And she was too nervous to try relighting the fire with Fred sleeping right next to it.

Fred was still snoring away as Emba dragged

herself up onto her feet, but there was no sign of Odolf. He must have been up even earlier than usual, gone to fetch more wood maybe, or to find a bush to wee behind.

Emba wiggled her shoulders and shook out her hands to get her blood flowing again, and then marched around the inside of the circle until she felt... well, not warm exactly, but a little less cold. Then she set off to find her own bush to wee behind—one of the few remaining ones she *hadn't* burnt down the night before—keeping an eye out for Odolf as she went. She tried calling for him too, shouting out his name into the thick fog, but there was no reply.

By the time Emba got back to the stone circle, she was starting to worry. She kept thinking about when Necromalcolm had stolen Fred away from the cave in the middle of the night, in order to lure Emba to his tower. What if the same thing had happened again? What if he'd sent his men for Odolf this time? What if they'd bound and gagged him before he could raise the alarm, and carried him off into the darkness? But unlike Fred's kidnapping, there was no note telling

Emba where to go if she wanted to save him. And no sign of a struggle either. No blood—thank goodness—or scuff marks on the ground. If someone (or something) *had* taken Odolf while she and Fred were asleep, they must have spirited him clean away... *Oh no*, thought Emba, staring round the circle in horror. What if the witches had got him?

There was one stone that was smaller and thinner than all the others. Was that there yesterday? A cold, sick dread pooled in the bottom of her stomach as she rushed over to examine it more closely. What if the witches' curse had spread to Odolf and he'd been turned to stone as well when morning came?

"Odolf," she cried, running her fingers along the rock. Could that jaggedy bump there be his nose? And those indents there, could they be his eyes—one sitting on its own and the other with a thin line of moss over the top of it, like an eyebrow? "Oh Odolf, is that really you?"

The stone didn't answer.

"I'm so sorry," said Emba. "It's all my fault. I should have woken up when it was my turn to keep watch.

I should have been ready with my fire to protect you. Oh Odolf," she cried again, wrapping her arms around her friend's stone shoulders and weeping into his thick, stone neck.

"Emba?" came Fred's croaky voice from behind. "What are you doing?"

Emba swung round with tears streaming down her cheeks. "It's Odolf. He's gone."

Fred's wrinkled brow grew even more wrinkled. "What do you mean he's gone? I just heard you talking to him now. 'Oh Odolf,' you said."

"I d-don't mean he's gone, *physically*," Emba explained through choking sobs. "Q-quite the opposite in fact. He's not going anywhere anymore. Look at him!" Emba stepped back so Fred could see, pointing at the stone's strange, flattened face. "What are we going to do?"

Fred looked blank. "I don't see anything," she said. "Just a stone."

"Exactly! He's been petrified like the witches. The moon must have been full enough to break the spell after all. They must have caught him in the night when they came to life and used some weird witchy magic on him. And now he's been turned to stone along with them. *That's* why it's called the Stone Circle of Certain Doom."

Fred let out a loud splutter of laughter. "Oh Emba. Don't be so silly. That's not Odolf. And it's not a witch, either. It's just a lump of rock. They're *all* just lumps of rock."

"Well, where is he then? I woke up this morning and he was gone."

"He's probably gone to fetch some more firewood," said Fred. "I'm sure he'll be back soon."

Emba shook her head. "No, he's not collecting wood—I already checked. And he hasn't gone for a wee behind a bush either—not unless it's the longest wee in history. He's not *anywhere*."

Fred wasn't laughing now. "And you've tried calling for him?"

"Yes. Over and over. But either he's too far away to hear because someone's carried him off in the night, or he's too hurt to answer." *Or he's been turned to stone.* Emba wasn't sure which option was worse.

"Perhaps you should ask the Tome? Maybe one of the prophecies can tell us where he's gone."

"No. The Tome can only tell us what will happen to Odolf in the future. We need to know where he is now." Fred thought for a moment. "This is a job for the scrying bowl. I understand why you didn't want to use it before, Emba dear, but one look into the bowl won't turn you into your father, I promise. You'll *never* be like him."

Emba shook her head. "There's got to be another way," she insisted.

"Of course," said Fred. "We can sit here and wait, and hope he comes back. Or we can carry on searching for him. But if he *is* in danger…"

"Then every minute counts," Emba finished. She took a deep breath. And then another. "Alright," she said at last. "I'll do it. For Odolf. You'll have to help me though—I've never done anything like this before."

Fred pulled Emba into her chest, hugging her tight. "You're a good girl, Emba Oak. And a brave and loyal friend. *That's* why you'll never be like your father."

Fred gave her another squeeze for luck and then released her again. "Alright," she said. "The first job is to fetch some water for the bowl."

"That bit should be easy," said Emba. "I left it out in the rain last night, along with the goblet, so we'd have some fresh water for breakfast." She hurried back to their pile of belongings—to her goatskin bag and the Tome of Terrible Tomorrows. To Necromalcolm's scrying bowl and his horrid, jewelled blood-collecting cup... except there *was* no cup.

"The goblet!" she cried. "It's gone. Whoever's taken Odolf must have taken that as well."

"But not the bowl?" said Fred, hobbling over to join her. "That's strange."

"The bowl's still here," Emba confirmed, trying to keep her worries in check. "And it's full of rainwater."

"Perfect," said Fred. "Now then, I *think* all you have to do is stare into the bowl and focus your mind on the person you want to see. I mean *really* focus, until there's no room for anything else in your head."

That shouldn't be too hard, Emba thought. Her head was already full of Odolf and what might have befallen him. But no matter how hard she stared into the water, nothing happened. The only thing reflected in the water was her own face.

"Don't get distracted with thoughts of where he might be," advised Fred. "Or whether he's hurt. Focus on his essence."

His essence? Emba wasn't sure she even knew what that was. She thought about the sweet-smelling essence of Juneflower that Fred distilled each summer for her heart cures, and the pungent essence of purgeweed that she used for her stomach-cleansing draughts. The smell alone was enough to clean out most people's stomachs. Did that mean she needed to focus on Odolf's smell as well as his appearance? Sort of woody and damp, with a touch of cheesy feet and wild garlic breath?

"I see him!" Fred cried out suddenly. "He's fine!"

"I don't," said Emba, screwing up her whole face with the effort and staring at the scrying bowl until her eyes began to water. "I can't see anything."

"No, not in the bowl. Behind you."

Emba turned to see Odolf wheeling a huge, wooden

wheelbarrow towards them, grinning from ear to ear. "Morning!" he called out. He came to a halt at the stone ring and reached into his barrow, emerging with a beautiful golden-crusted loaf of bread. "Your breakfast awaits."

Emba didn't know whether to hug him or shout at him for scaring them like that. "Where were you?" she demanded. "I thought something terrible had happened. I thought..." She stopped, biting down on her lip. It was probably best if she *didn't* tell him how she thought he'd been turned to stone. She'd never hear the end of it otherwise. "It doesn't matter *what* I thought," she finished. "You should have told us where you were going."

"You were asleep," Odolf protested. "I didn't want to wake you. Besides, I didn't mean to be gone so long. I only went to fetch some more berries—I was really hungry after all the extra warrior training I did last night to help keep me awake—and I borrowed the jewelled cup to collect them in style. I was hoping to collect enough for breakfast too, to surprise you with. But then I bumped into an old pedlar on his way to market and we got talking. He agreed to swap the cup for his barrow so that Fred doesn't have to walk all the way to the Petrified Peaks."

Fred reached a gnarled hand towards him, as if to stroke his hair. But it wasn't a comforting stroke she was aiming for. It was a worm. A fat, juicy tree worm that seemed to have set up home on top of Odolf's head.

"And I see you've collected some bait for us too, on your travels," said Fred with a grin, holding the plump, wiggling creature by its tail. Or its head. It was hard to tell. "I know the perfect fishing spot on the way to Hibbert's Hill..."

"Let me guess," said Emba, already picturing the next round of dangers lying in store for them. "Is it the Shrieking Stream of Soul-Crushed Sorrow? The Remorseless River of Roaring Rage? The Loathsome Lake of Liquified Limbs?"

Fred looked confused. "Liquified limbs? Of course not," she said. "I'm talking about the Pretty Pond of Peace and Pleasantness. A lovely spot, teeming with big, fat fish. But we don't have to stop there if you don't want to."

"No, that sounds perfect," said Emba quickly, her mouth already watering at the thought of freshly cooked fish. "Let's go!" But then she stopped and looked around, as a horrible thought struck her. "You didn't tell the *pedlar* we were headed for the Petrified Peaks, did you?" she asked Odolf. "You didn't mention anything about *me?*"

"With half the county out looking for us, you mean, hoping to claim the duchess's reward? Of course not," he said, looking hurt. "I was very discreet, although he seemed too nice to turn us in anyway. He even threw in a cloak and a loaf of bread. I thought the cloak might come in handy as a disguise for you, to cover up your scales."

Emba felt bad for doubting him. It seemed like Odolf had learnt his lesson after telling Necromalcolm's henchmen where to find her before. "Thank you," she said. "You're right, I'll be harder to spot with a cloak covering my arms and legs."

"And we'll get to the Pretty Pond of Peace and Pleasantness twice as fast with the barrow. You did really well," Fred chimed in, although her left eye was twitching again. "But perhaps we should get going all the same and eat our breakfast on the way. The stone circle won't offer us much protection now that it's daylight."

"Yes," agreed Odolf. "We need to get out of here. I didn't tell the pedlar anything, but he told *me* something. He said he'd just passed a group of bounty hunters looking for a pair of wanted criminals. Apparently there are posters plastered all over the nearby villages."

Fred's eye twitched again. "Just as I feared," she said quietly. "The sooner we get to Howard's, the better."

Chapter 11

The Surprisingly Pretty Pond of Peace and Pleasantness

Progress was much quicker with Fred, the tree worm and everyone's belongings bundled up inside the pedlar's barrow, and the children taking turns to push. The thought of bounty hunters on their tail helped to speed the party on their way too. But despite the constant threat of discovery, Emba felt altogether more hopeful as they wheeled their way along the rutted lanes. The fog had finally lifted and the morning was cold but sunny, with dew drops twinkling in the grass like jewels. She felt altogether fuller too, thanks to the delicious breakfast of bread now sitting in her stomach, not to mention warmer. The pedlar's cloak was a little scratchy and musty-smelling, but Emba was glad of it all the same.

Fred seemed in better spirits too, now that they were on their way again, despite being squashed up in a barrow with her leather-sandalled feet sticking out the end, gnarled toenails pointing up to the heavens. Once she'd finished giving out directions she settled into the journey, telling tales of her hermiting adventures with Howard as she bumped and jiggled along. There was the time Howard fell into a pit of angry wasp snakes and couldn't call for help because of his vow of silence, and the time an equally angry wasp snake got stuck inside one of his down-filled pillows. And then there was the time Fred bumped into a *really* angry wasp snake in the dark of Howard's hut, jabbing it with one of her toenails. It wasn't quite clear from the story whether the snake was already angry to start with, or if it was the jabbing that had made it so cross. But what *was* clear was that the wasp snakes around Hibbert's Hill had some serious temper problems.

"Are there a *lot* of wasp snakes around Howard's hut?" Emba asked, her hopeful mood fading at the thought. If there was one thing Emba Oak hated, it was snakes sneaking round in the dark (or in the light, come to that). Snakes hiding in pillows sounded even worse. And as for pits of angry hissing snakes... She shuddered at the very idea.

"Oh yes," said Fred cheerfully. "Hundreds of them. But don't worry, they're easy to spot with their yellow stripes, and they're completely harmless. Well," she corrected herself, "*mostly* harmless anyway. As long as you don't make them cross. And you'll know when they're cross because of the buzzing noise they make. Other snakes hiss, but wasp snakes buzz."

Emba shuddered again as she imagined her pillow, wriggling and buzzing under her head. Eek! Maybe she *wasn't* in such a hurry to reach the safety of Hibbert's Hill after all. She pulled her new cloak tighter around her shoulders and vowed to practise her fire-breathing again when she got the chance. A burst of flame would see off an angry wasp snake, wouldn't it? Or would that only make it crosser? She was about to ask Fred's advice on the matter when something caught her ear... a rustling in the undergrowth behind them. She spun round in fright, but there was no one there.

The same thing happened again a few minutes later,

with another rustling sound. Emba's scales prickled as if someone was watching them, but when she turned back to check, the path was as empty as before. Perhaps she'd imagined it.

"Fred," she hissed the third time it happened. "I think we're being followed." Emba checked behind her again, picturing a greedy mob of bounty hunters chasing down the path, ready to haul them back to the castle and claim their reward. Or maybe they'd hold them prisoner until the duchess's soldiers arrived, given that the reward was for information on their whereabouts rather than their actual capture. But thinking about soldiers dragging her and Odolf back to the castle was no less terrifying. And what about Necromalcolm? Would he be there at the castle too, waiting for Emba and her precious dragon blood?

Odolf paused with the barrow, listening hard. "Are you sure?" he said, sounding nervous. "I can't hear anything."

"No," agreed Emba. "I can't either now," she admitted. "But there was definitely someone there. I didn't just hear them, I *sensed* them too."

"Perhaps it was a bird," said Fred. "Or a rabbit."

"Or another one of your dragons," suggested Odolf.

"I'm sure it's nothing to worry about," Fred added. "If it was soldiers acting on a tip-off, they'd have caught us by now."

"I suppose so," agreed Emba. She stole a glance at Fred's left eye to see if it was twitching, but for once it was perfectly still. Maybe it *was* only birds after all. Maybe the tickly, prickly feeling under Emba's scales was just that—a tickle.

"Come on," said Fred cheerfully, changing the subject. "The Pretty Pond of Peace and Pleasantness is just the other side of those trees. Let's go and catch ourselves a fish."

The Pretty Pond of Peace and Pleasantness really *was* perfect. The blue water sparkled in the sun, and three fat fish jumped straight out of the water into the waiting barrow at the mere *sight* of the leaping tree worm dangling off the end of a twig. There were no signs of any bounty hunters or soldiers to detract from the idyllic scene. No sign of any lurking lizards. No hidden swamps. No stone witches. No red cracks in the sky or motherly dragon warnings. Just singing birds and a chance to rest their aching legs and top up their bellies. Emba found it *most* disconcerting. Danger had been hot on her heels for so long now, that the thought of finally letting down her guard and relaxing seemed all wrong.

She glanced around uneasily as the delicious scent of cooking fish filled the air, already bracing herself for the next dangerous encounter. But the sky stayed clear, the birds kept singing, and the ground stayed solid beneath her feet. It all seemed too good to be true. There had to be a catch somewhere. Maybe the Pretty Pond of Peace and Pleasantness was like the Pool of Perilous Perception, and if Emba gazed into its waters for long enough she'd see some dreadful, mind-tangling truth reflected back at her. Maybe *that's* where the danger lay. But no matter how hard she stared into its beautiful crystal-clear depths, all Emba could see was pretty pond plants. And more fish. And a perfect pink fortune frog, doing leisurely laps around his perfect, pink-flowered lily pad.

She crouched down at the water's edge to refill her sheep's bladder flask, bringing it up to her lips for a deliciously refreshing drink. It felt cool and healing as it trickled down her fire-sore throat. *Ah yes, that was better.* And then she stopped herself short, spitting an entire mouthful back into the perfect pretty pond. "This water," she asked, turning back to Fred, who was perched on a nearby rock, cleaning swamp mud out from under her long toenails with the help of a sharp stick and a large gum polish leaf. "Is it safe to drink?"

"Safe isn't the word *I'd* use," said Fred, sending a wave of panic through Emba's chest.

I knew *it was too good to be true,* she thought, sticking out her tongue and trying to scrape away the last traces of pond water with her finger. She imagined tiny invisible eggs already working their way through her body, getting ready to hatch into something disgusting: slimy stomach slugs maybe, or mini shrivel leeches. *Yuck, yuck, yuck.*

But Fred hadn't finished yet. "No, 'magical' is a much better word," she said. "A few mouthfuls of Pretty Pond of Peace and Pleasantness water is enough to cure all your aches and pains and worries. For a little while, anyway. And they say that if you sprinkle it in your enemy's eyes it can make them forget why they were attacking you in the first place. Again, it's only temporary, but handy in the middle of a fight."

Emba pulled her tongue back into her mouth. "Oh," she said. "Yes. That does sound handy. *Very* handy." She and Odolf could have done with some magic pond water on their previous adventures. It sounded like just the thing for battling magpikes and bears.

"No bathing in it though," Fred warned. "It can make you forget your worries and concerns so much that you never want to leave."

Forgetting all my worries sounds good to me, thought Emba, taking another long slurp from her flask, and then another and another. She drank until her belly felt wobbly and swollen with water, then topped up her flask again in case of any unforeseen fights along the next stage of their journey. There might not be any danger *here*, but that didn't mean it wasn't coming. It could be following along behind them even now, getting ready to strike when they least expected it.

Chapter 12

The Hushed Hermit of Hibbert's Hill

There *was* no danger following them though. Or at least if there was, it didn't choose to reveal itself. Emba still couldn't shake the feeling that someone, or something, was watching them—but that's all it seemed to be: a feeling. The rest of the journey passed completely without incident, apart from an impressive number of toilet stops. Maybe Emba shouldn't have drunk *quite* so much pond water after all. But at least she wasn't thirsty, which meant her flask stayed nice and full. It was still full when they finally arrived at Hibbert's Hill, and began the long, slow push up the slope towards Howard the Hushed Hermit's hut.

Emba had been expecting a small, wooden dwelling made of crudely sawn tree trunks. But it wasn't a wooden hut at all. It was a mud hut. A *huge* mud hut, with separate rooms for eating and sleeping and a room for quiet 'contemplation' (which was another word for 'thinking', according to Fred). It even had its own library, which was a first for Emba, with shelves of leather-bound books running right around the walls.

Howard was nothing like she'd imagined him either. Emba had assumed all hermits were short, round and old like Fred, with weathered, crinkly skin. She imagined they all had wild, grey hair and gnarled, yellow toenails that tapped against the ground when they walked. But Howard was tall and thin, with perfectly normal-looking feet and no hair whatsoever. He *did* seem quite old though, with wrinkles on his face that deepened whenever he smiled or frowned, or narrowed his eyebrows in a questioning fashion.

He had the most expressive face—and hands—of anyone Emba had met, using them in place of words with surprising effectiveness. Somehow she knew what he was saying, as he welcomed them into his home and showed them round, without a single sound leaving his lips. And when Odolf asked about the best

place to practise his hero training before dinner—
a question requiring a more complicated answer than
facial expressions and hand gestures could convey—
Howard didn't bat an eyelid. He simply pulled out
the long, sharp stick he kept tucked into the knotted
rope belt of his sackcloth tunic and drew out his
answer using stickmen and simple pictures on the dry
mud floor.

Odolf headed off straight away with his wooden
spear and a look of heroic determination, and a yawning
Fred took to a comfy bed and down-filled pillow for a
pre-dinner nap. Howard raised his eyebrows at Emba,
as if to say, 'What about you? What would you like to
do?' and Emba smiled shyly back at him.

"Would you mind if I took a proper look round your
library?" she asked. "I've never seen so many books
before." In truth, she'd only ever seen *one* book before:
The Tome of Terrible Tomorrows. Fred had taught
Emba to read by scratching out letters on the ground
using a sharpened twig—rather like Howard and
his stickman pictures—before moving on to simple
printed pamphlets she'd brought back from the market

about local trials and the latest public executions. At best, the pamphlets were boring, and at worst they were gloomy, grizzly and grim. They never made for *nice* reading. But books were different. Books could be about anything. The idea of entire *shelves* of them filled Emba with a fluttery feeling of excitement and possibility. What sort of weird and wonderful places and creatures might be lurking between the pages of one of Howard's leather-bound volumes? What exciting ideas might be contained within their covers, just waiting to be discovered?

Howard nodded, smiling a warm, 'of course you can, be my guest' kind of smile, and led Emba back to the library. He gestured with his hand, as if to say 'read whatever you like' and drew up a stool from the corner for her to sit on. Then he bowed his head in a friendly farewell and left her to it.

Wow, thought Emba, breathing in the heady scent of leather and ink. She examined the nearest shelf, running her finger along the spines. There were books with plain brown covers, and books with colourful dyed ones. There were books whose covers were so worn with age that the writing on their spines had rubbed clean away. As for the titles Emba *could* read… well, they *all* sounded good: *Magicke Charmes and Recipes* by Swindleforth Abercrombie; *A Quiet History of Hermits* by Thomasina Tacit; *Myths and Legends from the Land of Giants* by Maxwell Gargant; *A Guide to Ancient Druy and Other Vanished Beasts…*

Emba paused. *What on earth were ancient druy?* She examined the battered-looking book more closely. It was a small, neat volume, in a dark shade of red, with the title and author spelt out in thin, gold lettering along the spine. But unlike all the other books Emba had seen, this one didn't seem to be bound in leather. Its cover seemed altogether colder and shinier, and bumpier. Yes, when she ran her hand over it again it felt almost like… like *scales*. Almost like her *own* scales, in fact. The thought made her arms and legs tingle and sent a shiver of cold down her spine. But curiosity got the better of her and she pulled the book off the shelf, turning it over to see the cover.

"Oh!" said Emba, almost dropping the book in surprise. It wasn't a guide to ancient *druy* at all. It was a guide to ancient *dragons*. Some of the gold lettering must have worn away on the spine, but the title was still perfectly clear on the front. "A Guide to Ancient Dragons and Other Vanished Beasts," she whispered to herself, "by Lindorm Drake." Her hands were shaking as she turned to the first page and began to read:

The realm of dragons may be closed to mere mortals, but it wasn't always so. The ancient texts tell of great, fire-breathing beasts with thunderous wings, travelling through the sky's blood gash to seek out human knowledge in exchange for flame-forged gold. But the world grew too greedy for dragon riches and power, and foolish, grasping men sought to capture and imprison dragonkind for their own personal gain. Many paid for their folly with their own lives, but the dragon realm was not without its losses too—stories tell of two noble beasts who fell to earth and never rose again.

As the last of their blood drained into the soil where they lay, the sky sealed itself, the blood gash closing like a freshly healed wound. The seal proved impenetrable to all, save for a single day every twelve years—the span of time taken for a newly hatched dragon offspring to reach its full, fire-breathing majesty—when the forces holding the seal shut were at their weakest. And on that single day alone, it is said, can the seal be broken and a dragon summoned forth from its realm, if only for a few short hours, using the darkest of dark summoning magic. In all my travels and investigations, I have yet to meet a sorcerer who has successfully deciphered the ancient spells and completed such a summoning, although I believe there are those who have dedicated their lives to the attempt.

However, even the most powerful of ancient sorcerers have never entered the dragon realm themselves, and I believe no one ever shall. Indeed, I hope they never shall, for a mortal with such power— the power to break open the very sky itself and fly themselves up like a bird—would be a dangerous person indeed. Such a person could steal the dragon's source of immortality for themselves and become invincible...

Emba slammed the book shut again, breathing hard. *Twelve years*, she thought. *The span of time taken for a newly hatched dragon offspring to reach its full, fire-breathing majesty.* It was almost twelve years since *her* hatching. Was that why her scales had changed? Was that why she'd started breathing fire? And the red crack she kept seeing in the sky... that must be the breach between the two realms: *the blood gash closing like a freshly healed wound.* But according to the book, the seal between the human and dragon worlds could only be breached on one single day every twelve years.

That didn't make any sense. Emba had seen her dragon mother pass back through the crack twice now, on entirely different days. Unless... unless that was only the *spirit* of her mother. Maybe that explained why no one else except Emba—except someone of dragon blood—could see her. She remembered how Odolf and Fred walked straight through the middle of the dragon's belly on her first visit to the cave. She thought about her own hand passing right through her mother's claw when she reached out to touch her...

That wasn't my mother, Emba realised. *Only her spirit. Her ghost. Her soul.*

She sat down on the stool Howard had brought for her, feeling dizzy from so much new information. No wonder Necromalcolm had been so keen to get her blood and complete the spell that would give him the power of flight. He was planning to do what no one else had ever done before: to breach the dragon realm and steal their secrets for himself. To make himself immortal—too powerful to be stopped or defeated by man or beast. And the day of his great, evil plan was coming, wasn't it? The day that only came once every twelve years...

Emba opened up the book again and reread the introduction. It was clearly very old, and things had changed since Lindorm Drake had written it. Necromalcolm *had* deciphered the ancient spells, hadn't he? He'd completed his summoning, dragging Emba's dragon mother through the breach in order to steal her blood and give him the power of flight. And if his blood spell had actually worked, giving him wings instead of rooting him to the spot, perhaps he'd have made it to the dragon realm that very same day. But it *hadn't* worked—either because her mother's dragon blood hadn't been freely given, or because Necromalcolm had an attack of the hiccups halfway through an important part of the spell—and he'd been forced to wait another twelve years until he could try again.

The twelve years would be up soon enough though. It was only a matter of weeks now until Emba's birthday, which would usually be something to look forward to. Fred always marked the day with a special breakfast of duck egg pancakes and tangberry jam, and apple cakes for tea. But now the thought of her approaching birthday filled Emba with a sense of dread. If it really *was* the day when the seal between the two realms could be broken again, then Necromalcolm must be getting increasingly desperate. Desperate to regain his human form. Desperate to track Emba down again. And more desperate than ever to help himself to her precious dragon blood and harness the power of flight in time for the big day.

Chapter 13

The Bloodcurdling Buzz of Biting Rage

Emba sat in the library, lost in dark, fearful thoughts, until an angry buzzing noise from somewhere above her head brought her to her senses. She looked up to see a long, yellow-and-black-striped snake slithering along a row of books towards her, buzzing as it came. It didn't just *sound* angry, it *looked* angry, its mouth stretched wide to reveal a flickering forked black tongue and two enormous yellow fangs.

Emba leapt up from her seat in fright, sending the stool clattering onto its side. But she didn't stop to pick it up. She hurtled out of the library without so much as a backward glance and didn't stop running until she reached the bedroom.

"Fred!" she cried, flinging herself towards a snoring

hump of blankets. "Fred, wake up!"

The hump of blankets stopped snoring and let out a grunt of surprise. A head of tangled silver hair emerged, followed by a pair of anxious-looking, grey eyes. The left eye began to twitch. "Emba? What is it?" asked Fred, pushing back the blankets and hauling herself up—slowly and painfully—into a sitting position. "What's happened?"

"A wasp snake!" said Emba, throwing herself into the old woman's waiting arms. "It was in the library. I heard it buzzing and then I looked up and there it was, all slithery and stripy and horrible. You should have seen its fangs… it was going to bite me, I know it was."

"Hush now," said Fred, as Emba buried herself in her guardian's chest. "It's alright. You're safe here." She stroked Emba's hair. "You know what they say about wasp snakes…"

No, Emba *didn't* know what they say about wasp snakes. She'd never even *heard* of them until today.

"Their buzz is worse than their bite," finished Fred. "And when they're *not* buzzing, they can be quite friendly. Loveable even."

Emba wasn't convinced. It was hard to imagine anything with gleaming yellow fangs and a forked black tongue being lovable. "I didn't even do anything to make it angry," she said. "I was just sitting there thinking about my birthday, and Necromalcolm, when I heard it coming for me."

"Necromalcolm?" Fred's voice grew sharp. "What's he got to do with your birthday?"

"I found a book in the library," said Emba, holding it up to show her. "It's an old one about dragons."

Fred's left eye twitched harder as she studied the cover. "*A Guide to Ancient Dragons and Other Vanished Beasts* by Lindorm Drake," she read. "I don't understand. What's that got to do with your birthday?"

"Look at the first page," said Emba. "Then it will all make sense."

Fred opened the book and began to read, her lips moving soundlessly as her eyes scanned across the page. "Oh," she said at last. "Oh, I see. At least I think I do. You're worried that it's nearly twelve years since the seal between the two realms was last broken. And you think Necromalcolm is still planning on breaching the seal himself, using the power of flight, twelve years later. Which means he's still after your blood… that he's more desperate for it than ever."

Emba nodded, waiting for Fred to tell her that she was being silly. That there was no need to worry, because even if Necromalcolm *was* still alive, he was nothing more than a lizard now. And a mere lizard couldn't pull off a powerful spell like that. A mere lizard couldn't hurt her. But Fred didn't say any of that. She didn't say anything at all. She pulled Emba into an even tighter embrace and kissed the top of her head.

"It's true, isn't it?" said Emba. "You think so too."

"Maybe," admitted Fred. "I think you're right to be on your guard. But you'll be safe enough here," she said, "with all these wasp snakes buzzing round the place."

"Why?" asked Emba. "Is Necromalcolm scared of snakes too?" Maybe she'd inherited her fear from him.

"I've no idea," said Fred. "But I do know what a wasp snake's favourite food is: lizard."

There were no lizards on the menu at dinner that evening. Howard had prepared a delicious vegetable and chestnut dumpling stew, with baked goat's cheese and prickle herb scones. The smell was a hundred times nicer than the scent of the roast blue stench caps the night before, and it tasted even better than it smelled. Odolf polished off two big bowlfuls of stew (and five scones) in record time, declaring it the tastiest meal he'd ever eaten. Emba was surprised to find herself saying 'yes' to a second helping too. The scary new thoughts whirling round inside her head didn't seem to have affected her appetite.

Emba was *slightly* less worried about Necromalcolm sneaking up on her in lizard form, now that she knew he'd have all the wasp snakes on Hibbert's Hill chasing after him. And she was *much* less worried about one of the lizard-eating wasp snakes sneaking up on *her*, now that she'd remembered the flask of water she'd collected from the Pretty Pond of Peace and Pleasantness earlier that day. A few drops of that should be enough to calm down an angry snake long enough for her to escape. She'd already retrieved the flask from her bag and placed it next to her on the table, along with her scaring-off stone, to make sure she was ready.

The snakes kept their distance during the meal though. And there was no sign (or sound) of them after dinner either, while Howard and Fred were talking through the dangers that lay ahead on the journey to the Petrified Peaks. Not that Howard was doing any talking, of course. He was drawing out the various obstacles on the ground, using his special stick, while Fred interpreted them, with varied success:

"Hmm, that's a tricky one," she said. "Some sort of blanket, with a cloud and a skull... A bony weather blanket? No, wait, I've got it. A blanket of fog... Yes, a thick blanket of poisonous fog. Perfect!"

Hmm, thought Emba, yawning as she hooked a stray bit of prickle herb out of her teeth with her fingernail. *That doesn't sound particularly perfect to me.* And neither did the possibility of bandits, or the mighty shower of stones. But at least there was no mention of any swamps or witches. She yawned again, feeling tired at the thought of how much further they still had to go.

"Look at you," said Fred, catching her eye. "You're exhausted. I think we could all do with an early night. We've got a long day ahead of us again tomorrow."

Emba nodded and yawned some more. Now that she'd started, she couldn't stop.

Howard made everyone a warm cup of sweetly spiced goat's milk, and the weary travellers retired to bed. And oh, what a bed it was. The mattress was sinky and soft under Emba's back, and the down-filled pillow felt as if it was filled with air. *This is what it must be like to sleep on a cloud*, Emba thought as Fred tucked her in under her warm blankets and sang her nightly lullaby charm:

"Keep me safe in sleep tonight
From murderous tooth and claw,
From flashing blade and bloodied sword
And monsters bathed in gore.
Keep me safe from crunching jaws,
From eyes like burning coals,

Protect me as I dream tonight
From evil hearts and souls.
Keep me safe by moon, by sun,
Whenever danger calls,
Bind me from all harm and hold me
Safe within these walls."

And somehow Emba *did* feel safe, despite everything. Despite the dangers they'd faced already and the fresh dangers that lay ahead. Despite the thought that Necromalcolm would be getting more desperate—and therefore more dangerous—with every passing day. She felt for the flask of pond water she'd hidden under her pillow along with her stone, to make sure it was still there, and then she closed her eyes. She snuggled even deeper into the softness of her bed and let Fred's tuneless, warbling voice wash over her like a warm breeze, the words of the charm carrying her off to sleep.

Emba slipped back into the same dream as before. She dreamt of flying to the mountain and stepping inside the secret hidden door. She dreamt about the enormous bones rising up out of the ground and rearranging themselves into a dragon skeleton... a skeleton with a long, hooked claw, beckoning her into the swirling void of darkness beyond. And this time, Emba followed the dragon into the darkness— she didn't want to, but the pull was too strong to resist—and found another claw waiting for her inside, its sharpened tip glowing white against the blackness. And as she stretched out her hand to touch it, a terrible buzzing sound filled the air.

Bzzzzzzzz.

BZZZZZZZZ.

BZZZZZZZZZ.

It sounded like an entire nest of wasp snakes buzzing angrily in the darkness. Or maybe just *one* wasp snake buzzing right in her ear.

Emba jerked awake to find a pair of gleaming yellow eyes staring back at her. Her mind froze. All she could think about were those eyes and the matching yellow fangs below them. And the black forked tongue darting in and out of the wasp snake's mouth as if it was tasting the air... or getting ready to taste *her*. But then Emba remembered the flask of pond water tucked under her pillow and sprang into action. Actually no, that's not strictly true. Springing into action didn't seem like the best idea under the circumstances, with an angry wasp snake lying across her body. *Creeping* into action was more like it. *Easing gently* into action was the way to do it. Emba carefully moved her arm out of the blanket and slipped her hand under her pillow, reaching for the waiting flask.

There. So far so good. Easing out the waxed cork stopper with one hand was where things got difficult though. Every single tiny movement—every little jerk and wiggle—felt like it could be Emba's last.

Just stay still, Emba begged the snake, feeling the cork loosening with every twitch of her finger and thumb. *Don't move. Don't hurt me.*

The cork slipped out with a final *POP* and the snake's buzzing grew louder than ever. **BZZZZZZZZZZZZZZ.**

Its yellow eyes narrowed as if it was preparing to strike, and then...

...and then Emba whipped her hand forward, thrusting the flask in the snake's eyes and dousing him with pond water. The buzzing stopped at once and the snake drew its fangs back into its mouth. It looked more peaceful already. But Emba wasn't taking any chances. She tipped water all down its body, from the double tips of its black forked tongue to the end of its stripy tail, shaking out every last drop from her flask.

It worked! The wasp snake wasn't buzzing anymore. It was purring like a cat. Emba had never even heard of a purring snake before. The look of anger had gone from its eyes too. They looked kinder now, somehow—kind and dopey—and Emba could have sworn the creature was smiling. It tilted its head to one side, and then the other, before pulling away from Emba's face and curling up on her chest, tucking its head into its own scaly coils.

No, thought Emba. *Don't go to sleep. You can't stay there.* This wasn't how her pond water plan was supposed to go. The snake was supposed to forget about being angry and slither away, not set up camp on her chest and snuggle down for the night. Fred said the peace-bringing effects of the pond water were only temporary. What would happen when they wore off and the snake went back to its usual angry, buzzing self? The first thing it would see would be Emba, and she'd be right back where she started. But the snake had her pinned to the bed and, try as she might, she couldn't bring herself to tip him off onto the floor. What if the pond water wore off halfway through the attempt? If it had been angry before, it would be even angrier to find itself ousted from its comfy sleeping quarters and thrown to the ground.

Emba tried wriggling out from underneath it instead—she'd rather spend the night sleeping on the cold, hard ground than spend it wide awake and terrified in her nice warm bed—but the snake was too heavy. She was trapped. She couldn't even use her dragon's blaze to scare the creature off. At least not without setting light to the bed in the process.

"Fred!" Emba called, quietly, so as not to wake her new bed passenger. "Help me!" But Fred simply rolled over onto her back and began to snore. And there was no point calling for Odolf after that— he certainly wouldn't hear over the old lady's grunts and snorts and whistles.

"Mum," Emba whispered into the snoring, purring,

not-so-stillness of the night. "How about you?" But there was no answer from above either. No soft, beating wings. No giant shadow swooping down to scoop the snake up in its ghostly spirit claws. *No one* was coming to help, were they? Emba was on her own. In the dark. With a snake. Except somehow it *wasn't* dark, Emba realised as she lay pinned to the bed, trying to keep from crying. There was no light from outside. No light from the snuffed-out candle in the lantern. There was no light at all, and yet Emba could see the snake quite clearly. She could see the two sleeping humps of blankets in the beds beside her.

Emba remembered how bright the witch's circle had grown the night before, and how keen her eyesight had become as the fiery glow had filled her. She remembered how Fred had gasped out loud at the sight of her eyes—her dragon eyes. Had her eyes changed again? Was that the reason she was able to see so clearly? But yesterday she'd been possessed by fiery thoughts when the change had occurred. And now? Now her thoughts were cold and fearful and full of snakes. Perhaps it was something to do with the approach of her birthday: her coming of age. *Twelve years—the span of time taken for a newly hatched dragon offspring to reach its full, fire-breathing majesty.* Perhaps that's why the dragon changes were coming thicker and faster now, her body readjusting to each new power as it emerged.

What next? Emba thought, with a shiver that was part fear and part excitement. *Wings?* For a moment, she let herself imagine what it would be like: the gentle rip of skin as her soft leathery wings forced their way out beneath her shoulder blades, the soft cooling brush of air as they unfurled, stretching out to their full strength and beauty, and then...

No, she told herself firmly. *I'm only half dragon. I belong down here with Fred. And Odolf.* And as for the other half, the necromancer half, Emba didn't want to think about that. She didn't want to think about how the rain had appeared out of nowhere the night before, just when she'd needed it most. Just when she'd called for it...

She closed her eyes and tried to think of something nice instead. Nicer than Necromalcolm anyway. Nicer than the snake curled up on her chest, still purring away like a contented cat. She thought about the Pretty Pond of Peace and Pleasantness, with its sparklingly clear blue water and its plump silvery fish. Yes, that was better. She thought about the birds singing their melodic chorus, and the pink fortune frog, swimming round his lily pad. And the more deeply Emba imagined it all, the softer her pillow grew beneath her head, and the slower and steadier her breathing became. Somehow, as she lay there, remembering the cool, healing trickle of the pond water down her throat, she stopped worrying about the snake waking up and turning on her. Its gentle purring became a sound of comfort, rather than fear. And, before she knew it, exhaustion had taken over and Emba was asleep once more.

Chapter 14

The Flatulence of Fiendish Fate

Emba awoke next morning to a heavy weight pressing down on her chest, and a trio of anxious faces round her bed.

"You're awake!" cried Odolf. "Whatever you do, don't move. I don't mean to scare you but... THERE'S AN ENORMOUS SNAKE ON YOUR CHEST!"

The snake! Emba's breath caught in her throat as the events of the previous night came flooding back to her.

"Hush now, Odolf, that's not helping *anyone*," Fred scolded. "Morning, Emba dear," she added. "There's no need to panic. There *is* a snake on your chest, it's true, and he *is* a rather large one. But as I told you yesterday, their buzz is worse than their bite when it comes to wasp snakes."

"What about when they start purring?" asked Emba. "What does that mean?"

Fred listened for a moment. "Hmm, yes. It does sound more like a purr than a buzz now that you mention it. I've never come across that before. Have you?" she asked Howard.

Howard drew a finger across his mouth in a smile and then pointed to Emba and pressed his hands to his heart.

"It means he's happy? Really?" said Fred. "And he loves Emba? Are you sure?"

Howard nodded.

Emba wasn't sure she liked the sound of that. The happy part was fine—better a happy snake than an angry one—but she'd much rather he took his snakish affections somewhere else, thank you very much.

"But you don't even like snakes," observed Odolf, sounding a little envious. "I wonder why he chose you."

"Perhaps it's something to do with the soaking I gave him last night," said Emba. "He looked like he was about to bite me, so I used the water I'd collected from the Pretty Pond of Peace and Pleasantness to stop him attacking."

"Ah," said Fred. "Ah yes, I see. How many drops did you use?"

"The whole flask. Why? Was that wrong?"

"Not *wrong* exactly," said Fred. "But that's a lot of powerful water for one snake. I think you might have overloaded his system. It didn't just make him forget why he was attacking you, it's drowned out his attacking urge altogether—at least where you're concerned anyway." She tilted her head to one side and examined the snake more closely. "I think you might have got yourself a friend for life there."

"But I don't want a snake for a friend," said Emba. "Odolf's right. I hate snakes."

The wasp snake stirred on cue, lifting its head to gaze lovingly at her.

"H-hello there," said Emba nervously. "Thank you for not biting me. And for keeping me company all night. Do you think you could get off me now, though?"

Her heart almost stopped beating as the snake reared forwards, stretching out its horrid black tongue towards her face. *No!* The effects of the pond water must have worn off after all. *This is it*, Emba thought. *This is the bit where I find out how bad his bite* really *is compared to his buzz.*

But the snake didn't bite her. He licked her. He licked her nose like a faithful dog licking its master.

"That tickles," she whispered, trying not to wriggle. It felt light and fluttery against her skin.

The snake pulled his tongue back in and slowly uncoiled himself, slithering back down off Emba's chest and onto the floor.

"Oh thank goodness." She let out a long sigh of relief. "I thought he'd never go."

"Shh," teased Odolf. "You don't want to upset your new friend. Snakes don't normally lick people, you know. He must *really* like you."

"He's not my friend," Emba replied, pulling herself up into a sitting position so she could keep a closer eye on what the snake was doing. "He's just..." A sudden movement in the doorway caught her eye. "NECROMALCOLM!" she shrieked, as a big, green lizard scuttled out of the shadows.

It wasn't scuttling for long though. One moment

the lizard was there, orange eyes bulging at the sight of the wasp snake whipping across the floor towards it, and the next, it was gone. Emba caught the briefest glimpse of its back legs and tail as the snake held it tight in its jaws, half-in, half-out, and then they disappeared too.

"Wow," she breathed. "Did you see that?"

Odolf nodded. "*I* wouldn't want to be on the wrong side of your snake friend, that's for sure."

"I told you," said Emba. "He's not my..." But then she stopped herself. Maybe having a snake for a friend wouldn't be *so* bad after all. At least he'd keep the lizards away. She looked at the bulge slowly working its way down the snake's body. What if it really *was* Necromalcolm? What if all her troubles were over, just like that? "The lizard you saw crawling out the cauldron... was it a big green one like that? With bulging orange eyes?"

Odolf thought for a moment. "I don't really remember what colour his eyes were," he said, unhelpfully. "They just looked kind of lizardy and evil. You know?"

No, Emba didn't know. But she nodded all the same and turned back to the snake. "Thank you…" she began and then stopped, unsure how to address him. *Thank you, Snake*, seemed a little impersonal if they really were going to be friends. "Thank you… Whip," she said, recalling how quickly he'd whipped across the floor after the lizard. Yes, Whip the wasp snake had a nice ring to it. And Whip the sorcerer-slaying wasp snake sounded even better.

The time had come for the three adventurers to say goodbye to the cosy comforts of Howard the Hushed Hermit's hut. They were taking *some* comforts with them though: spare blankets, a plentiful supply of bread and apples and dry-cured strips of meat, plus fresh water and a batch of fig and honey cakes. Howard had also given Emba his copy of *A Guide to Ancient Dragons and Other Vanished Beasts*, which was tucked away in her now-bulging goatskin bag for safekeeping.

Emba was sorry to be going again so soon. Snakes and lizards aside, she'd felt safe at Howard's. Safer than being out in the open, anyway, hoping that an old pedlar's cloak would keep any passing bounty hunters from recognising her. She'd have liked to have spent more time exploring Howard's library too, but Fred had promised that they'd visit him again on the way back home, once they'd fulfilled the Tome of Terrible Tomorrows' cryptic prophecy.

Emba turned the Tome's words over in her head as they set off on the next arduous leg of their journey, up into the mountains, in case there was anything Fred might have missed. Anything about hiding somewhere safe and warm until after the day of danger—her twelfth birthday—had passed:

Evil stirs beneath the scales,
As sleeping forces wake,
As fleshless bones begin to glow
And stony mountains shake.
A treasure lost ere long is found
By one who heeds the call
Of secrets under stony spines

Within the hidden hall.

But there was no mention of safety. Or staying warm. Or birthdays. No, the Tome wanted 'the one', whoever that was, to 'heed the call', and so that's what the three of them were doing. Four now, if you included Whip.

Of course, Odolf, being Odolf, still thought *he* was the chosen one, being called to recapture his lost treasure in the shape of his dragon belt buckle. But, after the last few nights, Emba wasn't so sure. Could the sleeping forces be the giant dragon bones from her dreams? They were certainly fleshless, and they *were* waiting inside the stony mountain. In which case, maybe it was *her* they were calling. Or perhaps she'd been right before. Maybe the sleeping forces were the new powers awakening inside of Emba herself, along with the 'evil'—her father's blood—stirring beneath her scales? Oh, it was no good. Her head ached already from thinking about it. Why did the Tome always have to talk in riddles?

She pulled out her new dragon guide to see if that might offer any helpful clues, reading as she walked along, which was no easy feat.

"Look, it says here that dragon's scales are impervious to fire," she said, showing the book to Fred, who was tucked up back in her barrow. "What does impervious mean? Is that a good thing or not?"

"It means they're completely resistant to fire," explained Fred. "Fire would have no effect on dragon scales."

"Like when I picked up that burning branch," said Emba. "It didn't even feel hot against the new scales on my hands." She carried on reading. "It also says dragons are prone to sore gums. Do you think I'll get those as well?" She ran her tongue around her mouth, searching for any rogue patches of pain. Her gums felt fine though. She read on. "And it says... oh no. I don't want to think about *that*." She snapped the book shut again, but there was no shutting out the fears whirling round inside her brain again.

"What?" asked Odolf. "What does it say?"

"It says dragons are immortal," Emba told him with a shiver. "That's why Necromalcolm wants to harness the power of flight and seize control of the dragon realm. It's all part of his plan to make himself live forever." The necromancer had been dangerous enough when he was rooted to the floor of his own tower, and twice as dangerous when the spell had set him free. How much worse would he be with the power of flight at his command, safe in the knowledge of his own immortality? And how long would it be before he enslaved the whole of mankind *and* dragonkind to do his bidding?

Whip began to buzz loudly as he snaked along the ground beside her, as if the thought of Necromalcolm finding a way to live forever had upset *him* too. Either that, or the effects of the pond water had finally worn off and he was getting ready to test out his fangs on a nice fleshy part of Emba's foot.

"Shh, it's alright, Whip," said Emba soothingly. "We won't let Necromalcolm win," she promised. Saying it out loud made it sound as if it was true. "He might be a powerful sorcerer, but he can't complete his precious flight spell without more of my blood. All we have to do is stay out of his way until after my birthday and then it'll be too late. The breach between the two realms will be closed for another twelve years."

Whip's buzz grew softer, almost as if he understood what Emba was saying.

"Good boy," she added, as if she was addressing a dog. She drew the line at stroking him though.

"I didn't even realise he was still with us," said Fred, twisting round in her barrow for a better look. "Snakes don't usually like to leave their familiar habitat. Mind you, I've never heard a snake purr before either. I guess that makes him special. Or just very confused."

"He must be getting tired now though," Odolf pointed out. "Maybe he'd like a ride in the barrow with Fred. And maybe you'd like to push for a bit," he told Emba. "*I'm* getting pretty tired too."

"Of course," agreed Emba. "If that's alright with you, Fred. Would you like that, Whip?" she asked the snake, pointing to her guardian's lap.

Whip looked from Emba's face to the waiting wheelbarrow and back again. And then, with a very un-snakelike nod of agreement, he slithered up into the barrow and curled himself into a ball on Fred's lap like an enormous stripy, scaly cat.

"I'll hold your dragon guide for you while you're pushing," Odolf offered. "I can read it out to you as we go."

Emba was oddly reluctant to hand the book over. It felt like handing over all her deepest, darkest secrets— secrets she hadn't even discovered for herself yet. But the feeling was too hard to explain, and she *did* want to find out more about her dragon heritage. Maybe there'd be some tips on how to control her dragon's blaze too. "Alright," she said, passing the book to Odolf and taking up the barrow handles with a grunt of exertion. Fred had been heavy enough on her own, but Fred and Whip together plus the extra supplies from Howard felt like very hard work indeed. "No laughing though," she warned. "*I'm* part-dragon, remember."

"No laughing," agreed Odolf, looking hurt at the very suggestion. "I wouldn't dream of it."

He was as good as his word, to begin with. But then, there was nothing particularly funny about the average length of a dragon's claw or the number of bones in a fully grown tail. It wasn't until Odolf reached the section on dragon digestion that the corners of his mouth began to twitch.

"Ugh!" he cried. "Listen to this. Ancient sources compare the scent of a dragon passing wind to the smell of rotten eggs and fermenting fish guts. A single blast of dragon flatulence, the sources tell us, is powerful enough to knock a child clean off their feet." Odolf sniggered. "No walking behind you after a big meal then."

Emba glared at him. "I *said* no laughing."

"Yes, I know. I'm sorry," Odolf replied, smothering another giggle. "There's nothing funny about farts. We all do them, after all. Your dragon farts are just a little more dangerous than everyone else's… a little more likely to cause permanent injury to anyone caught in the backdraft."

"Hush now, Odolf, that's enough," piped up Fred from the wheelbarrow.

Buzzzzzzz, buzzed Whip, raising his head to glare at Odolf, yellow fangs bared.

"Alright, alright, I'm sorry," said Odolf, apologising again. "No more fart facts, I promise. And no more jokes. What about dragon burps? Do you want to hear what Lindorm Drake has to say about them?"

"Odolf..." warned Fred.

Buzzzzzzzzzzzzzz, agreed Whip.

Emba settled for another steely glare, determined not to give in to her growing annoyance and anger this time. That was how accidents happened. Big, fiery accidents.

"No burps. Got it," said Odolf. "Although, according to this, you might want to steer clear of cabbage in the future," he added. "Cabbage and dragons are *not* a good mix, apparently. Not for the dragon and definitely not for anyone standing within a twenty-yard radius. And speaking of tummy troubles, wait 'til you hear what it says about dragon diarrhoea..."

"Stop it!" roared Emba, unable to keep her anger in check any longer. "I said no laughing." That's what she meant to say anyway. But she could already feel the flames rushing up inside of her, so she clamped her mouth shut and swallowed hard, focusing on the coldest thoughts she could think of. The biting chill of fresh snow beneath her bare feet... The broken-off icicle Odolf had dropped down her clothes during dinner the winter before... No, that wasn't a good one. Remembering that made her even crosser. *Back to snow... to cold crisp snow.*

Yes, that was better. The wild rush of fire retreated back down into Emba's belly, with only the tiniest ribbon of flame escaping out of her left nostril and scorching the back of the wheelbarrow. It was nothing compared to the terrible fire she'd started on their night at the stone circle. It was enough to put a stop to Odolf's antics though. He leapt back in fright, screeching like a cat with a trodden-on tail.

"I'm sorry," he said. "I didn't mean it. Any of it. I guess..." He looked down at his feet. "I guess I'm just a bit jealous."

Emba blinked in surprise. "Jealous? Of *me?* Why on earth would you say that?"

"Because *I'm* supposed to be the hero forged in fiercest flame," said Odolf, quietly, referring back to the Final Prophecy. "I'm the one who's supposed to heal the chasm with my blood and make everything right again. But *you're* the one with all the amazing powers. I don't even have my belt buckle anymore and you... you've got protective scales that make you impervious to fire. You've got special eyes that help you see in the dark—I read about them in your book too—and you've got your own fiercest flames waiting inside you, ready to blast your enemies with. If anyone's a hero here, it's you."

Emba shot her friend a sympathetic smile. "I'd swap every one of those powers with you if I could," she said, although she wasn't completely sure that was true anymore. The dragon part of her seemed to be growing stronger every day now, and perhaps that part of her liked the feel of her protective scales and the burning heat in her belly. But she wasn't ready to admit that to Odolf. "Seriously," she said. "I'd be happy for you to have my dragon powers. Especially the dragon farts," she added with a less-than-serious wink. "You're more than welcome to those!"

"That's enough of that sort of talk from *both* of you," scolded Fred. "I suggest you put the book back in your bag, Emba. You'll need all your wits about you once we hit the narrow mountain path. From what Howard told me, I'd say the hardest part of the journey is still to come."

Emba glanced back over her shoulder at the mention of the word 'journey', struck by the same strange feeling she'd had on the way to Hibbert's Hill—the feeling that someone, or something was following them. But there was no one there.

Chapter 15

The Rattling Rockfall of Ruin

Emba's sense that someone was following along behind them, unseen, didn't go away this time. It grew stronger still as she heaved and panted her way up the first winding stretch of mountain path. Whip seemed to feel it too. He'd left the comfort of Fred's lap to wrap himself around Emba's neck and shoulders (much to her nervous horror), like a thick, scaly scarf. Her newfound tolerance of snakes did *not* extend to wearing them. Every now and again, he'd stretch out his neck to peer back over Emba's shoulder, as if he was checking for unwelcome strangers too, buzzing softly to himself.

"What is it, Whip?" Emba whispered, too scared to turn her head and look for herself. She didn't want to risk jogging the wasp snake with any sudden movements. "What can you see? Is there anyone there?"

It was Odolf who answered though. "Maybe he spotted another lizard," he suggested unhelpfully, turning round to check. "But if he did, it's gone now. One look at Whip and it would have scuttled off pretty quick, I'd have thought, unless..." Odolf stopped himself just in time, but Emba knew exactly what he'd been going to say: *unless it's Necromalcolm.*

There was a sudden noise from behind. A noise like someone kicking a stone. *Bandits! Bounty hunters! Necromalcolm!* Emba's head was a panicked tangle of thoughts as she swung her entire body round to see, remembering about the snake around her neck but forgetting about the barrow handles clenched tight in her fists. The wheelbarrow swung round with her, lurching towards the edge of the narrow path and setting off a mini rock fall below.

"EMBA!" shrieked Fred above the clatter of falling stone, her voice shrill with fear.

The old woman's knuckles showed white through her leathery skin as she clung to the edges of the barrow, beads of sweat glistening in the deep wrinkles of her face.

Emba couldn't see the danger at first. "What?" she asked nervously. "What's wrong?"

"The wheel!" Fred gasped.

Emba's eyes widened in horror as she caught sight of the front half of the barrow's wheel. There was nothing underneath it anymore—nothing but empty air and a steep drop down to a grizzly, bone-breaking end below.

"Quick! Help me get it back onto the path," Emba yelled to Odolf, all thoughts of bandits and bounty hunters forgotten as she braced herself to pull Fred to safety. Odolf was there in an instant, taking hold of the handles with her. "We'll need to lift up first to get the back half of the barrow off the ground," said Emba. "But only a tiny bit. And then we pull. We pull like crazy. Got it?"

"Got it," agreed Odolf. "Odolf Bravebuckle to the rescue!"

"One, two, three, *pull!*"

They pulled so hard that the wheelbarrow shot

backwards, knocking the pair of them flying. But Emba didn't care. She didn't care about the sharp stones digging into her bottom or the sharp end of Odolf's elbow digging into her ribs. Fred was safe. That was all that mattered.

"I'm so sorry," she told her guardian, scrambling back onto her feet. "I should have been concentrating harder. Are you alright?"

"I think so," said Fred shakily, patting herself to check. "Yes, still in one piece as far as I can tell. No harm done."

Emba wasn't ready to forgive herself yet though. "You could have *died*," she said, still reeling from the possibility. "I should have been looking where I was going instead of worrying about someone following behind us." She glanced towards the crumbling edge of the path and the dizzying drop below. "One tiny push further and you'd have been gone. *Gone*," she repeated.

Fred clambered slowly out of the barrow and pulled Emba into her arms. "Hush now," she said. "You stopped in time, that's all that matters. And then you saved me. That's the part I'll remember. You *and* Odolf. Thank you," she added, opening her arms for a moment to pull Odolf into her embrace as well.

"I can't let my imagination run away with me like that again though," said Emba. "I need to focus on the task at hand. I mean, if there really was someone following us, they'd already have attacked us by now..." She broke off at the sound of a voice coming from behind them. It sounded like... yes, it sounded like someone calling for help. "Did you hear that?" she asked the others. "Or am I imagining that as well?"

"I heard it too," said Odolf, craning his head to see round the bend in the path.

"Help!" came the voice a second time, closely followed by a girl. A girl with long black hair and a dirt-streaked face, who came stumbling and panting up the path towards them. "Please help me," she begged, her dark eyes swimming with tears. "There's an angry arachnomercy after me."

"What's an arachnomercy?" asked Odolf. "And why's it angry?"

"It's a giant, killer scorpion with two tails and a

famously bad temper," Fred began to explain. "It looks a bit like—"

"That," interrupted Emba, pointing down the path towards a black, hard-shelled creature with eight legs, two sting-tipped tails and a vicious, snarling mouth of razor-sharp teeth. It was the size of a small dog, with snapping, crab-like front claws, and was scuttling towards them at an alarming speed.

Her first instinct (which she was heartily ashamed of afterwards) was to back away, fast. Emba Oak hated scorpions even more than she used to hate snakes, and this was no ordinary scorpion. It was a vicious-looking, drooling beast of a thing. No wonder Whip was buzzing at top volume, staring down the path at the new arrivals with his fangs bared and his tongue flickering in and out like crazy. Emba's second instinct was far less cowardly though. She reached into her goatskin bag for her scaring-off stone and got ready to fight. *And if a sharp missile to the creature's head doesn't stop it in its tracks*, she thought, *then perhaps a burst of flame might do the trick.*

There was no need for either, as it turned out. Odolf

was already on the case. He snatched up his wooden spear from the barrow and sprang into action. "Odolf Bravebuckle to the rescue!" he roared, racing past the exhausted girl to face the arachnomercy head-on. "Get away from her, you big brute!"

The arachnomercy let out a blood-curdling screech that made Emba's scales tingle. All four of its red eyes swivelled on their eye stalks as it turned its attention to Odolf, both tails curling up into the air as if it was preparing to strike.

"Watch out!" Emba cried.

Odolf didn't falter for a moment though. He lowered his head like a charging bull, raised his spear and ran towards the creature at full pelt. The arachnomercy screeched a second time, eyes blazing with anger as the double tails came whipping over its head with its spiked stingers extended. Emba could hardly bear to watch. But Odolf swerved to the side at the last moment, ducking down with his spear and jabbing it in under the creature's low-slung body. And then, with a mighty grunt of effort, he flicked the arachnomercy up into the air, sending it flailing backwards towards the edge of the path.

For a moment—although it felt longer to Emba, watching on in terrified disbelief—the creature seemed to hang there, upside-down, its legs flailing uselessly, and then it was gone, screeching down the side of the mountain out of sight.

"Woah!" she cried, running over to Odolf and throwing her arms round him. "That was amazing. *You* were amazing."

"Yes," agreed the girl, drying her tears. "Thank you so much. I don't know what I'd have done without you. I got ambushed by a gang of scary bounty hunters, looking for some children, and ran straight into an arachnomercy's nesting ground in my rush to get away. That thing's been chasing me ever since."

"Bounty hunters?" Emba let go of Odolf and turned to face the girl, relief turning back to fear. "Where were they?"

"By one of the mountain streams down there," said the girl, pointing over her shoulder. "I don't know where exactly. I was already lost when I started running, and now…" She looked like she was going to cry again.

"There, there," said Fred, putting a comforting arm around the girl's shoulders. "You're safe now. Where was it you were trying to get to? Maybe we can help."

"I'm supposed to be going to the Petrified Peaks to look for yellow curewell flowers for my aunt. She's dreadfully sick," the girl explained, "and our neighbour said the flowers would help."

"You mean yellow curewell *roots*," said Fred. "The flowers don't have any healing powers."

"Really?" The girl let out a long, shuddering sigh. "I'm so useless at this. I don't know what I'm doing and I don't know where I'm going. I couldn't bear to see her like that though—fading away before my eyes. I had to do *something*. I had to try."

"We're on our way to the Petrified Peaks too," said Emba, raising her voice over Whip's buzzing. Even with the arachnomercy gone, he was still noisy. "You can come with us, if you want. I'm Emba, by the way. And this is Fred and Odolf."

"Huh-hum," said Odolf, making a funny noise in his throat. For a moment, Emba thought he must have swallowed a fly but then she realised what the problem was.

"Sorry," she added. "I meant to say this is Fred, the Wise Hermit of Witchingford Wood, and this is Odolf Bravebuckle, the er... the Brave Warrior of Witchingford Wood. And this is Whip, my wasp snake. You'll have to excuse the buzzing. He does that a lot."

"I'm Merle," said the girl. "And oh, yes please. I'd love to join you. Thank you."

"Why don't you take my place in the barrow and rest?" Fred offered as the party prepared to set off again. "I can walk for a bit."

"No, no, I'll be fine," insisted Merle, setting off up the path. "I feel better already now that the creature's gone. Now that I'm not on my own anymore."

"If you're sure. Come on then, let's go," said Fred, clambering back into the wheelbarrow. "Before those bounty hunters catch up with us. They sound like trouble."

Chapter 16

The Saved Stranger's Stone

Merle seemed determined to put a brave face on things, despite her worries about her aunt. She must have been exhausted after her brushes with the bounty hunters and the arachnomercy, but she managed to keep up with Emba and Odolf, showing polite interest in their quest. Fred had developed a nasty cough which made conversation difficult though. Every time Emba started to tell Merle about the Tome of Terrible Tomorrows, Fred would start hacking and spluttering, rendering any further attempt at explanation pointless. The further they travelled up the steep, winding path, the steeper and more winding it became, and the less breath they had left for talking anyway. Eventually, the conversation ran out altogether, to be replaced with wheezing pants and grunts of exertion.

"Stop!" cried Fred, breaking the new silence that had settled on the group. "Look!" she cried, leaning forwards in the wheelbarrow to point at a scrubby patch of leaves.

"What?" asked Emba and Odolf in unison.

"Trotterstem," said Fred, her face alight with excitement, "for making toenail balm. Let's stop here for lunch and I'll gather some for my herb collection. There should be enough here to keep me going for the next three winters."

Odolf didn't need telling twice. He set down the barrow with a thump and flopped onto the nearest rock. "Good idea. The bit about lunch, I mean. I need to keep my strength up for when we reach the Petrified Peaks. Who knows what heroic challenges I might have to face to reclaim my dragon belt buckle?"

"You can cross 'mighty shower of stones' off Howard's list of possible dangers," said Emba, helping Fred out the barrow. She was thinking about the clattering rockfall she'd created when she swung the wheel off the path. "We've done that one already. That just leaves poisonous fog and bandits. Although perhaps he meant bounty hunters instead," she added, with a quick glance over her shoulder.

"He didn't say we'd *definitely* come across all those things," Fred said. "They were simply dangers to be aware of. We might be lucky and have a clear run all the way to the Petrified Peaks." She wasn't coughing anymore but Emba noticed her guardian clutching at her chest as she bent over to pick the trotterstem leaves.

"You sit down with Odolf and let me get those for you," Emba told her.

Fred smiled gratefully. "Thank you, Emba dear. Why don't you join us, Merle?" she added, patting the rock beside her. "Have a rest and tell us all about yourself."

"There's not much to tell," said Merle, squeezing onto the rock beside Fred and Odolf. "It's just me and my aunt. She's all I've got left in the world and now she's... she's..." She sniffed, dabbing at her eyes. "How long do you think it will take us to get there?" she asked, changing the subject.

"Another day or so," said Fred. "It's not far in terms

of distance, but the path gets even steeper from here. Too steep for the barrow, unfortunately, which means I'll have to walk. Don't worry though," she added, patting Merle's arm. "I'm sure your aunt's in good hands with your neighbour, and curewell roots are good for all sorts of ailments. Perhaps if you tell me more about her illness, I can recommend some other herbs that might help? Like swellbalm or wild hexbell, for example, or slippery sootheblossom."

"Hexbell?" said Merle, jumping up. "I think I spotted some of that back there. I'll go and check," she added, hurrying off down the path.

Emba watched her go. "She's very brave, isn't she?"

"*She's* very brave?" said Odolf. "*I'm* the one who defeated the arachnomercy single-handedly."

"Hmmm," said Fred, with a twitch of her left eye. "I hope that's *all* she is."

Emba turned to her in surprise. "What do you mean?"

"I don't know exactly, just a funny feeling in my toenails when I touched her arm. And your snake doesn't seem to like her much. His buzzing gets louder every time she comes near."

"Don't take any notice of him," said Emba. "He's always buzzing about something, aren't you, Whip?"

The wasp snake didn't respond. He *had* stopped buzzing, she realised, but that was probably because he was asleep. Yes, that would explain it.

"Well, *I* think Merle's nice," Emba added, coming to her new friend's defence. It wasn't like Fred to be suspicious, especially not of a child. Merle couldn't be much more than a couple of years older than Emba herself. "Your toenails must be wrong this time."

"Wrong?" said Fred sharply. "My toenails are never wrong."

Emba changed tack. "Please," she begged. "Just give her a chance, that's all I'm asking. I don't get to meet many people my own age, living in a cave in the middle of the woods. And those I do meet usually treat me like I'm some kind of freak. But Merle's different. We could be friends—*good* friends—I know we could."

"Hmmm. Alright," said Fred at last. "Just be watchful around her until we get to know her better. And I'd rather you didn't discuss the Tome of Terrible Tomorrows with her either."

"Alright," promised Emba. "Can I go and help her look for hexbell leaves now?"

Fred's left eye gave a double twitch. "I suppose so. But do be careful, Emba dear. I mean it."

"Don't worry, I've got my scaring-off stone in my bag and a giant snake round my neck. I'll be fine." And with that Emba hurried off down the path after Merle before Fred could change her mind.

She'd only gone a few yards when she spotted a clump of distinctive grey, furry hexbell leaves peeking out from a gap in the rocks. But there was no sign of Merle. Emba stared around in confusion. Where was she?

Buzzzzzzzzzzzz, buzzed Whip, lifting his head up and looking around with her.

"Can you see her?" Emba asked. "Which way did she go?"

The snake said nothing. No surprise there. But Emba could hear a voice coming from behind a large nearby rock. A soft, murmuring voice. Could that be Merle? She edged closer, peering round the corner.

It *was* Merle. But she must have been talking to

herself—mumbling, rather—because there was no one else there. *Strange.* In fact, she seemed to be talking into her own hand, which was even stranger. Emba crept a little closer still, trying to make sense of what she was seeing. There was something *in* Merle's hand. A stone of some kind, by the looks of it.

BUZZZZZZZ, buzzed Whip. A sudden, loud buzz that made Merle spin round in surprise.

"Emba!" she cried, a flush of colour rushing to her cheeks. "What are you doing here?"

"I came to help you look for hexbell leaves," said Emba. "I found the leaves, but I couldn't find you. And then I heard you talking… Not that I was eavesdropping or anything," she added quickly. "I couldn't actually hear what you were saying." It was true. Merle had been talking much too quietly for Emba to pick out any words.

Merle's blush deepened. "How embarrassing. I was just talking to my charm," she said, opening her hand to show Emba the grey stone. It was perfectly round and smooth, with a neat hole through the middle of it. "It's… it's something my aunt gave me. For luck. The *last* thing she gave me, in fact, before I set off for the Petrified Peaks." She shook her head. "You must think I'm an idiot, talking to a stone, but it makes me feel closer to her, somehow. It makes me feel less scared and lonely."

"Oh Merle," said Emba, treating her to her best sympathetic smile. "I don't think you're an idiot at all. I know exactly what it's like to feel lost and alone. When Odolf left me on my way to Gravethorn Castle, it was the worst feeling ever. I didn't know if I'd ever see Fred again either. But I did," she said. "Odolf came back for me and we saved Fred together. You'll find your yellow curewell roots and save your aunt, I know you will. You'll be together again soon. And in the meantime, you've got us."

Merle smiled back at her. "Thank you. I hope you're right. You won't tell the others though, will you? About the stone. I wouldn't want them to think less of me."

They wouldn't judge you. They're not like that. That's what Emba was *about* to say, when she remembered Fred's surprising warning. Perhaps her guardian wouldn't be so understanding after all. "Of course not," she said instead. "Your secret's safe with me. I promise." But even as she said the words out loud, she felt a tiny twinge of worry. Keeping secrets from Fred felt wrong. Emba had always shared everything with her guardian. And what if Fred's toenails were right? What if there *was* something suspicious about Merle? But it was too late now. A promise was a promise.

Buzzzzzzzzzzz, buzzed Whip. *Buzzzzzzzzzzzz, buzzzzzzzzzzz, BUZZZZZZZZ.*

"I'll leave you to it, shall I?" said Emba, trying not to let her anxiety show in her voice. "I'll pick the hexbell leaves and let you talk to your charm in peace and quiet."

"Thank you," said Merle again. She looked so grateful that Emba felt her worries melting away again. No, there was nothing suspicious about Merle. She was just a poor soul in need of kindness, that was all. And she'd been kind to Emba too. She'd seen the scales on her arms and legs when she'd taken off the pedlar's cloak earlier and she hadn't said anything.

She'd accepted Emba for who she was, without questions. It was only fair that Emba did the same for her.

She left Merle to her private thoughts and headed back up the path to Fred and Odolf, picking the hexbell leaves on the way.

"Where's Merle?" said Fred, with another twitch of her left eye. "I thought you were going to pick those together."

"She needed a private moment to herself." Technically speaking, that wasn't a lie, Emba told herself. It felt like one though.

"Hmmm," said Fred, sounding far from convinced, her left eye still twitching. But that's all she had to say on the subject. It seemed to be her new favourite word. "Hmmmmm."

Chapter 17

The Sleep-Sucking Swirl of Slumber

It wasn't only Fred who had a problem with Merle. Odolf clearly wasn't keen on her either. He turned moodily quiet during lunch, his ready smile replaced by a sullen scowl. And the more interest Merle showed in Emba, the more sullen his scowl became. Not even Howard's fig and honey cakes could cheer him up.

"What's up with you?" hissed Emba, when Merle excused herself to go to the toilet. "Don't you like her?"

Odolf shrugged. "She's alright, I suppose."

"Well, try being a bit nicer to her then. She's missing her aunt and could really do with some friends." Emba smiled inside at the word 'friends'. Odolf had been the only friend she'd ever known until now. Visitors to the cave came to see Fred, not Emba. They came for one of Fred's healing potions, or to consult the Tome of Terrible Tomorrows. They didn't come to see strange-looking girls with yellow-hazel eyes and scaled arms and legs. And when they *did* see Emba they treated her with suspicion and fear, rather than kindness.

But Merle was different. She thought Emba's scales were pretty—she'd told her as much over lunch. And she seemed genuinely impressed by the way they'd kept her safe from fire. And she liked Emba's eyes, and the fact that they helped her see in the dark. It made a nice change to be admired, rather than feared or made fun of, and Emba was only too glad to share her experiences with such a willing listener. It felt good to have a new friend too—one who *wasn't* a snake. A friend who didn't wrap themselves round Emba's neck and buzz into her ear. Not that Whip was doing either of those right now. He'd taken himself off onto a nearby rock to soak up some wintry sun and was being nice and quiet for once.

Odolf's scowl deepened. "She seems a bit nosy to me," he said, "with all those questions she kept asking about your scales, and whether you had any other dragon powers."

"You're just jealous," said Emba. "Because she's more interested in me than you." The accusation sounded meaner out loud than it had in her head, and the hurt look of surprise in Odolf's eyes made her feel meaner still. But that didn't make it any less true. Odolf *was* jealous of Emba. He'd already admitted it. He was jealous of her new powers and now he was jealous of all the attention she was getting from Merle too.

"Hush now, the pair of you," said Fred. "No squabbling. We're a team, remember. And Merle's welcome to join our team providing her intentions are genuine and she's telling us the truth."

Of course Merle's telling us the truth, thought Emba. *Why else would a girl be all alone in the mountains, if she wasn't fetching healing herbs for her sick aunt?*

"I don't trust her," said Odolf, stubbornly. "She reminds me of the duchess."

"The duchess?" repeated Emba. "Don't be ridiculous."

"Hmmmm," said Fred, who'd never even met the duchess. But then she stopped hmmming and started trembling instead. "Oh no," she murmured, staring over Emba's head with a sudden look of fear. "I hope that's not sleep-suckers."

"Sleep-suckers?" repeated Odolf. "What are they?"

Fred's eye began to twitch wildly. "They're bad news," she said. "*Very* bad news. We need to get out of here while we still can."

That didn't tell Emba much. "Why? What do they do?" she asked, craning her head round to see. But there was nothing there. Only the empty mountain path and a pretty wisp of mist swirling across the cold, clear blue of the sky.

"They release a soporific vapour to send their victims to sleep and then feast on their flesh while they're busy dreaming," said Fred, hauling herself up onto her feet with unusual speed.

Emba didn't know what 'soporific' meant—something to do with making people sleepy, presumably—but she *did* know what feasting on flesh meant. And she didn't like the sound of *that* one little bit. She leapt up too, sending precious cake crumbs flying off her lap onto the ground.

"What does one of these sleep sucker things look like?" asked Odolf, reaching for his spear.

"I'm not sure," said Fred. "It's too small to see."

That doesn't sound too terrible, Emba thought. Like being bitten by a mosquito during the night, maybe. Or finding a nest of cave weevils in your bed.

"But I can tell you what a *swarm* of sleep-suckers looks like," Fred added. "Like that." She pointed to the silvery wisp of mist, drifting up the mountain path towards them. It was larger now though. Less of a wisp and more of a cloud. A thick, swirling cloud of fog. And it was still growing. "Oh my," she said, putting her hand to her heart. Her left eye was twitching like mad. "I've never seen a swarm like *that* before. There must be thousands and thousands of them. Enough to strip a man down to his bare bones," she added.

The poisonous fog, thought Emba, her heart beating faster. *This is what Howard warned us about.*

"How do we stop them?" asked Odolf. "What do we do?"

"You run," said Fred, "and you keep on running."

That's when Emba knew they were in serious

trouble. Fred hadn't run anywhere in all the years she'd known her. She wasn't even sure the old lady was *capable* of running.

"Run and save yourselves," cried Fred. "While you still can. Leave me and go. Hurry!" The fog seemed to fill the whole sky now.

Leave you? Emba stared at Fred in horror. "We're not going anywhere without you," she said. "Are we, Odolf?"

But Odolf didn't answer. He just yawned. A big, bear-like yawn that made Emba feel like yawning too. And once she started yawning, she couldn't stop. She closed her eyes for a moment as she tried to remember what they were talking about. Something about running... or was it sleeping? Yes, sleeping, that was it. And now her eyes were closed she found she didn't really want to open them again. She wanted to sit back on the ground and rest for a moment. No, she wanted to lie back down on the ground. Yes. That was better. *I'll just lie here for a moment*, Emba told herself, *and then...*

...and then...

…and then nothing.

Emba found herself back at the secret crypt under the mountain as sleep overtook her, the giant dragon skeleton beckoning her into the blackness with its long, gleaming claw. She found herself walking into the darkness to find a second gleaming claw fixed into the wall. And when Emba pressed the tip of her finger to the sharpened point of the waiting claw, a trickle of blood ran down into a big crack in the floor below.

"Emba!" someone shouted in the darkness behind her as the crack began to spread. As the very walls of the chamber began to tremble and shake.

"Emba!" they called again. "Shake up!"

Emba was already shaking. Everything was shaking.

Or was it "*Quake* up!" they were shouting? Emba was already doing that too. Shaking and quaking and watching in horror as the trickle of blood from her finger became a stream and the crack in the floor became a gaping chasm waiting to swallow her whole.

"EMBA!" The voice was louder than ever now. A girl's voice. "EMBA, WAKE UP!" She felt a hand on her shoulder, shaking her hard. It was a *real* hand, not a dream hand. And the voice... that wasn't in Emba's dream either. Her eyelids felt like they'd been stuck down with honey, but Emba forced them open all the same, dragging herself back into consciousness.

She gazed groggily at the blurry face staring back down at her. And then, as the face eased itself slowly into focus, Emba saw who it was. Merle.

"Thank goodness," said Merle. "I wasn't sure you were going to wake up. You have to help me save the others. You have to use your dragon's blaze."

"My what?" Emba's mind felt like it was full of wool. Soft, sleepy, warm wool.

"Your dragon's blaze," repeated Merle. "I managed to roll you to safety but Fred and Odolf are still in there." She pointed to the thick swirl of fog behind them. "You have to use your fire to save them. To scare away the sleep suckers before it's too late."

"Huh?" Emba was trying to focus, she really was. "Odolf and Fred are in trouble?" she repeated groggily, forcing herself to sit up.

"Yes," said Merle. "Big trouble. You need to start thinking angry thoughts. You need to get that fire going."

Odolf and Fred... in trouble... angry thoughts...
Emba screwed her face up tight, fighting the urge to
shut her eyes again and sink back into warm, velvety
sleep. *Angry thoughts. Angry Necromalcolm thoughts.*
She forced herself to remember those final, awful
moments in the basement of Necromalcolm's tower,
when the necromancer had blasted Odolf back against
the wall and left him for dead. She remembered how
the fire had risen up from her belly in fury, roaring out
of her mouth in a burst of flame. Emba could feel it
again now, building up inside of her, as she recalled
Necromalcolm's response: "Come back," he'd shouted
as Emba rushed to her friend's side. "You're spilling
your precious blood on the floor. You're wasting it."

A fierce stream of flame came bursting out of
Emba's mouth at the memory, blasting into the cloud
of sleep-suckers. For a moment, the cloud seemed to
grow rather than shrink, as wisping clusters fled in
different directions to avoid the scorching heat, and
then the entire swarm began to retreat as one. The fog
was rolling back across the sky now as quickly as it
had arrived.

"Keep going," said Merle. "It's working."

Emba couldn't keep going though. Her anger was already cooling, giving way to fear. What if she was too late? What if Fred and Odolf were already nothing but a pile of bones? But as the last of her flame flickered and died, Emba dropped her gaze back down to the ground and saw them: two slumped figures with their flesh still firmly on their bones, and a stripy coil of scales curled up beside them.

Thank goodness!

"Fred!" Emba called as she hurried over to them. "Odolf! Wake up!"

Nothing happened.

No one moved.

"Fred!" Emba cried, crouching down beside her beloved guardian and shaking her by the shoulders. There were angry red bites all over the old lady's face, hands and feet, but she was still breathing. Breathing very heavily, in fact. Fred let out a loud pig-like snort, and then rolled onto her back and began snoring. Odolf was equally covered in bites and equally impossible to rouse, so Emba fetched one of the spare flasks of water from the barrow and squirted it onto his face.

There was a shuddering gasp of shock as the cold hit his skin and Odolf's eyes flew open.

"Wh-wh-what was that?" he stammered, patting at his wet cheeks. "Wh-where am I?" He sat up and stared around in confusion.

"You've been asleep," said Emba. "We all have, well, apart from Merle," she added, wondering how her new friend had managed to escape. "There was a swarm of sleep-suckers and Fred told us to run and then... and then I don't remember anything after that. Merle saved me though—I know that. And then I used my dragon's blaze to blast the sleep-suckers away and threw some cold water in your face."

"Thank you," said Odolf, groggily. "Thank you for saving me. And for the cold water... I guess." He gave her a sleepy smile.

"Oh Odolf," Emba cried, throwing her arms around his neck. "I'm sorry for what I said before, about you being jealous. I didn't mean it. I'm glad you're alright. Now we just need to wake Fred."

But there was no need. Fred let out another mighty

snort and her eyelids jerked open. "My toenails!" she cried. "Don't let them take my toenails!"

"Shh, it's alright," said Emba, stroking her guardian's poor, bitten face. "It was only a dream. No one wants your toenails."

"A dream?" repeated Fred. She scratched at one of the bites on her nose. "The sleep-suckers... yes, I remember now. What happened?"

"Emba scared them off with her fire," said Odolf.

"And Merle helped too," added Emba, keen to prove to Fred that her new friend *could* be trusted after all. "She was the one who woke me up. If it wasn't for Merle, we'd still all be fast asleep, getting chewed by sleep-suckers." She put a hand to her own face and felt a cluster of sore bumps under her fingers. They must have been feasting on her too. "It's a good job Merle was here, wasn't it?"

"It certainly was," agreed Fred. "Thank you." But then her eyes narrowed. "Wait a minute, how did you manage to fight your way through to rescue us without falling asleep?" she asked.

Merle shrugged. "I don't know. I didn't even stop

to think about that. I just charged straight in. Perhaps it was the herbal ointment my neighbour gave me to keep away the mosquitos and pinch ants?"

"Hmmmm," said Fred, looking far from convinced. "Perhaps."

Chapter 18

Magic, Mystery and Merle

They were a good few hundred yards further up the path when Emba remembered about Whip. She'd been so relieved to see Fred and Odolf back on their feet that she'd forgotten about the still-slumbering wasp snake, curled up on his rock. For a moment or two, she considered carrying on to the Petrified Peaks without him. After all, it wasn't as if Emba actually *liked* snakes. But then she thought about how far he was from home, and how keen he'd been to follow her into the unknown, and guilt got the better of her. Guilt and maybe a teeny tiny bit of fondness for his familiar buzz and excellent lizard-catching skills.

"I can't just leave him there," Emba told the others. "He'll be all confused when he wakes up. I have to go back for him."

"I'll come with you," said Merle.

"No, *I'll* come with you," said Odolf.

"I offered first," Merle protested.

"But I've known Emba longer," countered Odolf. "*And* I've known Whip longer. He likes me more, I can tell."

Emba looked at the pair of them and sighed. Why couldn't they just get along? "I don't need anyone coming with me," she said. "It's not far. I'll be back before you know it."

She left them to their bickering and hurried back down the track to look for the wasp snake. He roused himself at her approach and tucked his head onto one side, as if to say 'there you are.' And then he slithered over to meet her and twisted himself round her ankles in greeting, purring softly.

"I'm sorry I left you," said Emba, feeling a surprise rush of affection for him. "I won't do it again. I promise." She reached down her hand to him and he slid straight up her arm, coiling himself back around her neck and shoulders as if he belonged there. And, in a funny way, it felt like he *did* belong there. "Come on then," she told him. "We'd better get back to Odolf and Merle before full-scale war breaks out. It's a pity I don't have any more of that magic pond water left— I could do with some for them."

They were still arguing when Emba caught them up again. "Stop it!" she told them, fizzing with frustration. "If you can't say anything nice, then don't say anything at all."

It was a rather quiet journey after that. Quiet and slow, with Fred hobbling along on foot and the path growing ever steeper. The children took it in turns to carry the scrying bowl and the remaining food supplies, which were now bundled up inside one of the blankets and tied to the end of Odolf's spear. The Tome of Terrible Tomorrows was too heavy and precious for that though. Fred insisted on carrying that herself, despite Merle's offers of help.

The air grew colder the further they climbed, which did little to improve anyone's mood. "It's a pity you can't magic us up a bit more sun," joked Odolf, as the first patches of snow appeared up ahead. "Like you did with that rain."

"You can summon the weather?" said Merle, sounding impressed. "Amazing! I'd love to see that."

Emba shook her head. "No, it was a coincidence, that's all. I just happened to be wishing for rain when it started. Nothing happened when I wished for it to stop again. Besides, I'm not interested in magic. Not *that* kind of magic anyway. In summonings and scrying bowls, I mean. I only like the kind of magic Fred does—*good* magic that actually helps people."

"But there's no harm in exploring your powers and discovering your potential," Merle insisted, her eyes glittering. "Just think what you could do with magic at your command." She pointed to a small, stunted tree, with bare, spindly branches stretching low along the ground. "Like covering that tree with fresh leaves and fruit. That wouldn't hurt anyone."

"No," agreed Emba, "but…"

"And think of the animals who'd be able to eat the fruit," Merle added. "And the insects who'd grow fat and happy munching its leaves."

Emba was almost tempted for a moment. If she

really did have magic in her veins, perhaps she *could* learn how to use it for good rather than evil.

"Look, Emba already told you she's not interested," cut in Odolf, even though he was the one who'd brought up the subject in the first place. "She's worried she'll end up like her father."

"What's so wrong with that?" asked Merle. "I want to be like my uncle when I grow up."

"Your uncle?" Emba blinked in surprise. "I thought you said it was just you and your aunt?"

There was an awkward pause. "Yes," said Merle at last, looking pained. Her shoulders drooped. "It's only the two of us now. But I've heard plenty of stories about my uncle. He sounds like an amazing man."

"I'm sure he was," said Emba. "I'm sorry, I didn't mean to make you feel bad. I'm sure he was kind and selfless and brave, just like you. But Necromalcolm's none of those things. He's..." She searched for the right words.

"Ambitious?" guessed Merle. "Powerful?"

"No," said Emba. "I mean yes, he's both of those things. But he's also cruel and selfish..."

"…and a lizard," finished Odolf.

And intent on taking over the dragon realm and making himself immortal, Emba added silently. "Luckily, my snake's an expert lizard-catcher," she said out loud. "If Necromalcolm wants my blood, he'll have to outrun Whip."

Merle made a strange choking noise and Emba looked at her in surprise.

"What's wrong?" she asked. "Are you alright?"

"Swallowed a fly," Merle gasped, patting at her chest. "Yuck. Is that true?" she asked, once she'd recovered. "Would Whip really try and eat Necromalcolm if he got the chance?"

Emba nodded proudly as the snake purred up at her. "Yes, you'd save me, wouldn't you, boy?" she said.

Whip's tongue flickered in and out on cue, as if he was listening. As if he had proper ears and could understand what she was saying. And then he twisted himself round to face Merle, buzzing again. Merle flinched, drawing back with a worried expression.

"What's wrong?" Emba asked a second time. "Don't you like snakes? I didn't either until I met Whip."

"They're alright, I suppose, it's just…" Merle blushed. "It's just the thought of someone trying to hurt you. I know we've only known each other a short while but you already feel like family to me."

Emba could feel her own cheeks reddening with embarrassment too. But it was a good embarrassment— the embarrassment of a compliment that was so nice it left her stuck for words.

Merle's blush deepened. "Sorry. You probably think I'm crazy."

"Yes," said Odolf, treating her to a fresh glare.

"Of course not," said Emba. "It's a lovely thing to say." She reached out her hand to touch the older girl's arm. "I feel the same way too."

You already feel like family to me. Emba carried those words with her all through the long afternoon, basking in their warm glow as the air around her grew colder and darker. As the frosty atmosphere between Merle and Odolf intensified. By the time they set up camp for the night, on a small rocky plateau beside a trickling mountain stream, Emba was starting to lose patience with Odolf again. He was the one who was jealous. He was the one who kept finding fault in everything Merle said, with no thought to how worried she must be about her aunt. And when Merle offered to fetch some firewood, he almost knocked her over in his rush to push past.

"That's *my* job," he said, bristling with indignation. "Mine and Emba's. You can stay here and keep Fred company."

"Of course. I just need to pop to the toilet first," said Merle. "You'll have to excuse me." She hurried off into the gathering gloom in search of a quiet spot away from everyone else. But Emba had seen the grey stone tucked inside her hand and could guess where she was *really* going. She was off to 'talk' to her charm again, wasn't she?

It must have been a long talk because Merle still wasn't back when Odolf and Emba returned with the firewood. Fred must have fallen asleep waiting for her, snoring softly to herself with her head lolling on her shoulder.

"Perhaps she's constipated," said Odolf. "Or perhaps the toilet was a cover story. Perhaps she's busy plotting."

"Plotting?" repeated Emba. "What on earth would she be plotting?"

Odolf shrugged. "I don't know. How to worm her way even further into your good books? How to get rid of Whip? I saw the way she was looking at him earlier. Like she wanted to throw him off the side of the mountain."

Buzzzzzzzz, said Whip, who was curled up next to Emba's goatskin bag.

"I know she's all on her own and I'm supposed to feel sorry for her," said Odolf, "but she doesn't seem that worried about her aunt to me. And she told us she was searching for yellow curewell flowers, when Fred says it's the roots that have healing powers."

"So? She already admitted that she doesn't know what she's doing," said Emba, coming to Merle's defence. "Plus she'd just been chased up the mountain by bounty hunters and an arachnomercy, so she probably wasn't thinking straight."

Odolf didn't seem convinced. "And how did she manage to avoid the sleep-suckers using a simple insect ointment? There's something funny about her, I know there is. Why else would she go running off to the toilet to avoid talking to Fred? Because she's worried she'll say something silly and give the game away."

"Or because she's got a bad tummy and she's too embarrassed to admit it," Emba protested. She couldn't tell him the truth about the charm Merle's aunt had given her. A promise was a promise.

Odolf shook his head. "No," he said stubbornly. "She's up to something."

"Like what?"

"Like… like…" Odolf shrugged again. "I don't know. It can't be anything good though, can it?"

Chapter 19

The Sickening Serpent

Dinner was a subdued affair. The jaw-grinding chewiness of the dried meat strips didn't allow for much talking, and Emba was still too upset with Odolf to say anything anyway. Afterwards, when he offered to be first up on guard duty again, Emba simply nodded and retreated back into her own dark thoughts. And when Fred offered to sing her usual lullaby charm, Emba turned her down for the first time ever.

"No, thank you," she said, feeling oddly embarrassed in front of Merle. "Perhaps just sing it in your head tonight." What would the older girl think of her, still being sung to sleep at almost twelve years of age?

Almost twelve years. The mere idea of her approaching

birthday was enough to send Emba's thoughts spiralling again. She thought about Necromalcolm coming for her blood… about what would happen if he succeeded in breaching the dragon realm and stealing the secret of immortality. She thought about his sister, the duchess, and the reward she'd offered for information on their whereabouts, and she thought of all the dangers they'd faced on their journey so far. And then she thought about Merle, who'd been nothing but nice and kind to them all, and how Odolf was acting as if *she* was a danger too.

He's wrong. We can *trust her. I know we can*, Emba told herself, trying to ignore the sound of Whip's buzzing in her ear. He'd been buzzing ever since Merle got back from her 'toilet trip'. Emba Oak had listened to enough tales of magical warnings and omens round the fire to know that they should never be ignored. But this was a buzz, not an omen, she told herself stubbornly. A simple snake buzz, not a sign of approaching disaster. Perhaps Whip was jealous, just like Odolf, and that's why he kept buzzing whenever Merle came near. *She saved our lives*, Emba argued, silently. *If it wasn't for Merle, we'd still be stuck in that cloud of sleep-suckers having our flesh chewed.*

The idea of flesh-chewing insects was no less horrific than before, but Emba wouldn't have minded a sniff or two of their soporific vapour to help her nod off. Sleep had never seemed further away. The ground under her back was too hard and the thoughts in her head were too loud and tangled. And although she wouldn't admit it, even to herself, Emba missed Fred's soothing lullaby charm. She lay cold and uncomfortable, listening to the buzz of Whip in her left ear and the gentle, rhythmic breathing of Merle in her right. But then Fred started up with her snoring again—her full-blast night snoring—and all other sounds were drowned out.

Just as Emba was finally, *finally* starting to grow sleepy, she felt something brush past her foot. She opened her eyes with a start, blinking in the darkness. Then her dragon sight kicked in and Emba saw a figure creeping towards Merle, carrying a lit twig from the fire as a torch. She saw the figure crouch down and start rifling through Merle's belongings.

A thief! she thought, stiffening with fear.

A short, skinny thief.

A short, skinny, ODOLF-shaped thief.

"What are you doing?" she hissed, sitting up and glaring at him.

Odolf jumped. "Emba!" he whispered in surprise, holding up his twig torch to see her better. "You're awake! I was just er... just..." He bit his lip as if he was trying to think of a convincing lie. But then he shook his head and told her the truth instead. "I was looking for proof," he admitted. "Proof that Merle's up to something. That we can't trust her."

"Proof that you're still jealous of her, you mean," said Emba. "Proof that she's a better and braver friend than you'll ever be."

Emba was almost as surprised to hear the words coming out of her mouth as Odolf was. Almost. She could see the shock in his face as he stared back at her—the shock and the hurt.

"I'm sorry," Emba whispered. "I didn't mean it. You're a good friend, Odolf, I know that really."

"But not good enough apparently," he said slowly.

"Not brave or brilliant enough for the great Emba Oak."

"No, no, that's not true," Emba insisted. "I'd be lost without you, Odolf, you know that."

"Do I?" he said, his bottom lip trembling. For a horrible moment, Emba thought he was going to cry. But perhaps it was simply the coldness of the night making his chin wobble. There was no way of telling, because he slunk back to his sentry post by the fire without another word, turning his back on her.

"I'm sorry," Emba whispered again. "Please, Odolf. I hate it when we fight."

But there was no answer.

Sleep, when it finally arrived, brought with it the same dark dream as before. The same beckoning bones inside the mountain crypt. The same curved claw waiting in the darkness for Emba's finger, and the same cold tail whipping and buzzing against her legs...

Wait, Emba thought as she struggled back towards

wakefulness. There was no whipping tail before. No frantic buzzing. She dragged her eyes open and sat up, sharply.

"Whip!"

The wasp snake was thrashing around on the ground beside her, beating his tail against Emba's shins.

"What is it, boy? What's wrong?"

He swung his head back towards Emba, a frothing green foam bubbling from his jaws.

"What happened to you? Don't worry, Fred will know what to do," she promised, hoping it was true. "Fred," Emba called, scrambling across the rocky ground to where her guardian lay snoring. "Wake up. Something's happened to Whip. I think he's eaten something bad. Something poisonous."

What if it was a lizard? An evil lizard with dark magic running through his veins?

Fred let out one last final snort as she jerked awake, wiping at the trail of drool on her chin. "Poisoned?" she repeated. "Who's been poisoned?"

"It's Whip. Please Fred, you have to help him." Emba was surprised to find she was crying. She'd grown fonder of him than she realised.

"Alright," said Fred. "Let's have a look." Emba guided her over to the writhing wasp snake, but it was too dark for Fred to see. Without thinking, Emba turned back to the dying embers of the fire, opened her mouth and let out a long blast of flame. There was no build-up of anger this time, no rage. She simply thought about the fire—about her *need* for fire—and out it came.

"Ah, that's better," said Fred as the flames brought fresh light onto the scene. "Now then, let's see what's been going on here. Oh my," she added, as Whip swung his head round to meet her. "You poor creature. You *are* in a bad way, aren't you? This calls for night lace. And lots of it."

"What does it look like?" asked Emba.

"It's a small red plant with lace-patterned leaves," said Fred, "which grows in the cracks between rocks. I saw some round here yesterday evening, I'm sure of it." She pointed to a gap between two craggy boulders, but there was nothing there save for a torn-off stump of red stalk.

Odolf was there too now. He came stumbling over to see what was happening, apologising for falling asleep on guard duty. If he was still angry and hurt after his row with Emba, he didn't show it.

"It doesn't matter about guard duty," Emba told him. "We need your help. We have to find some night lace leaves for Whip, to counter whatever it is he's swallowed."

"What do you mean?" repeated Odolf, dopily. "Has someone poisoned him?" He turned to look at the still-sleeping Merle, curled up under her blanket. "I think we can guess who."

"Not now Odolf, please," Emba begged him. "Help me find these leaves before it's too late."

But there were no leaves to find, no matter how hard they scoured the area. Every single night lace plant they came across had already had its leaves ripped from its delicate red stem, leaving nothing but a useless stump behind.

Whip's buzzing was growing quieter now and his thrashing less violent. But he seemed to be growing weaker rather than better, and his eyes were beginning to cloud over.

Emba closed her hands round the last wilted stump of red stem, willing it back to life, as if she could squeeze fresh growth into its poor bedraggled remains by the sheer power of her mind. Through sheer desperation. *Please*, she begged the dead plant, as if it could hear her. As if it could understand. *You have to help me save him.*

"*Empty stems, all dead and dried,*" she chanted out loud, the words creeping into her mouth, uninvited,

"*Find the life that's deep inside,*

Fire red and pretty lace,

Bloom again within this place."

Emba jumped as she felt something tickling at her palms, opening up her hands to see. And there it was—a bright, healthy night lace plant, with beautiful laced, red leaves.

That's impossible, she thought, staring at it in disbelief. But there was no denying the evidence of her own eyes: the plant had been dead and now it was alive.

"I've got one!" she called to Fred, holding it out to show her.

"So have I!" cried Odolf. "They're everywhere," he

added, pointing from one crack in the rocks to another.

He was right. Where once there'd been nothing but wilted stumps, now there were bright bushy plants. There was no time to marvel over it now though. No time to wonder at the magic that had occurred. Emba wasn't sure how much longer Whip could hold on for. She and Odolf gathered up the leaves as fast as they could and helped Fred mash them into a thick red paste.

"What now?" Emba asked, with a worried glance at the rapidly ailing wasp snake. "How do we get him to eat it?"

Fred shrugged her shoulders. "Ask nicely?" she suggested.

Emba rolled the paste round in her hands until it resembled a misshapen sausage and placed it on the ground in front of Whip. "Here, boy," she said. "You have to eat this. It'll make you feel better, I promise. Pretend it's a nice, juicy lizard."

The snake was too weak to move though. Too weak to reach out for the waiting cure.

"Don't worry, I'll help," said Emba. "Open your

mouth—can you still manage that?—and I'll pop it in."

Whip opened his jaws a little, his tongue lolling like a frayed bootlace.

"That's it, just a little bit wider," said Emba, trying to avoid the sharpened tips of his fangs as she steered the night lace towards his mouth. She should have been scared but she wasn't. She was too concerned about Whip to worry about herself.

"Well done," she said. "Now close your mouth and wait…"

The snake closed his mouth obediently, but nothing happened. Maybe he had to digest it first. Or maybe it was already too late. Maybe he was too weak to be saved.

"What now?" Emba whispered to Fred. "How will we know if it's worked or not?"

"We wait," said Fred, simply. "We wait and we hope. And in the meantime," she added, "we sleep. There's nothing more we can do for Whip tonight, and we've got a big day ahead of us tomorrow. A *very* big day," she added, glancing across at Merle, who'd somehow managed to sleep through the whole drama. "How about you snuggle down again—you *and* Odolf—and I'll keep watch this time. I can sing your charm for you too, if you're ready for it now."

"Oh, yes please," said Emba, "that would be good. I mean, I'm getting too old for it, really," she added, correcting herself, "but it would be nice for Whip. He'd like that."

Chapter 20

The Petrified Peaks

Emba awoke to the sound of purring.

"Whip!" she cried, as the snake's face loomed into focus. "You're alright!" He was better than alright, in fact. His once-clouded eyes looked clearer and brighter than ever, and his striped scales gleamed in the morning sun.

Merle was a picture of concern when she heard what had happened. "I can't believe I slept through it all. I'm so sorry," she said. "I must have had a delayed reaction to the sleepsuckers' vapour. I fell asleep the moment my head hit the ground."

Buzzzzzzz, buzzed Whip.

"It's fine," Emba told her, with a meaningful glance at Odolf—a please-keep-your-suspicions-to-yourself kind of glance. But Odolf refused to meet her eye. Perhaps he was still angry with her after what she'd said last night. She wouldn't blame him.

Odolf was quiet all through breakfast. He was quiet as they packed up their belongings and continued their slow journey up the ever-steepening path, refusing to be drawn into conversation. He was still quiet as they shuffled through the dark, narrow gully between two jutting rocks and...

"Woah!" he cried as they emerged blinking into the bright, wintry sunshine on the other side. "Look at that!" he called to the others, any attempt at quietness forgotten. "It's... it's incredible."

"Wow!" murmured Merle, her mouth dropping open at the wonder of it. "The Petrified Peaks. I can see how they got their name."

"Yes," agreed Emba, gazing wide-eyed at the view before them. "They really do look like the spiky spines on a dragon's back. Just like in my dreams."

"What dreams?" asked Fred. Her left eye began to twitch.

"I've been dreaming about dragon bones," Emba

explained. "About them calling to me, beckoning me into the crypt underneath the mountain."

Merle put her hand on Emba's arm. "You mean you've seen the door to the hidden crypt? Did you go in? What did you find? Tell me everything!"

"Why are you so interested in the crypt?" butted in Odolf. "How do you even know about it in the first place?"

"My aunt used to tell me stories about it," said Merle. "She said there was a hidden crypt underneath the mountain but nobody had ever managed to find the way in."

"It was pretty easy in my dreams," Emba told her. "I just—"

"Let's wait until we get there, shall we?" interrupted Fred. Her voice was sharp.

She still doesn't trust Merle, does she? thought Emba. *Not even after she saved our lives. Neither of them do.* "We need to find your herb first, anyway," she said out loud, as Whip buzzed in her ear.

"*My* herb?" Merle looked puzzled for a moment. "Oh, you mean the curewell flower for my aunt."

She dabbed at an unseen tear with her finger.

"The root," Odolf corrected her. "Not the flower."

"Yes, of course," said Merle. "I keep forgetting. That's why it's so lucky I found you all. I'd be useless on my own. I just hope I'm not too late to save her."

For a moment, Emba was tempted to try her luck with Necromalcolm's scrying bowl to check on Merle's aunt for her. But only for a moment. It hadn't worked before when she was looking for Odolf and, even if it did work this time, Emba was scared of what it might show her. What if her friend's aunt was already dead? How would she break the news to her then?

And if she did manage to master it this time, that would prove she was growing more like Necromalcolm. First there'd been the rain-summoning—what if it wasn't a coincidence after all?—and now the mysteriously resurrected night lace plants... It must have been the magic in Emba's veins that brought them back to life. Even in the cold light of day, there was no other explanation. It was her father's dark magic, flowing through her and it seemed to be getting stronger.

It was a slow final drag to the Petrified Peaks and Fred was really struggling now. Her breath was heavy and laboured and her left eye was twitching harder than ever. Looking at it made Emba feel quite peculiar.

Her guardian's eye wasn't the only twitchy thing though. Merle had grown increasingly nervous and jumpy as they neared their destination, checking over her shoulder every five minutes and jumping at each little sound.

"Are you alright?" Emba asked, catching a glimpse of the holed stone in her friend's hand. She must have been clinging on to it for comfort.

Merle's cheeks coloured. "What? Oh yes, sorry. I keep thinking about those bounty hunters."

"They won't have ventured this far," said Emba, with more confidence than she felt. But once the idea was in her head, she couldn't get it out again. As they neared the base of the mountain, the sense of being followed—of danger approaching—was back with a vengeance. She tried to distract herself by looking for

Merle's healing herb.

"There!" Emba cried at last, pointing to a patch of dusky yellow blooms beside a wizened tree stump. "Are those curewell flowers?"

Fred nodded. "Well spotted. That's a lovely big clump too—enough for a whole month's worth of medicine, if that's what you want," she added, with a sideways glance at Merle. "Pinch them underneath the bottom leaves and twist, and then the roots should come out easily."

"I'll help you," offered Odolf, chivalrously, dropping to his knees beside Merle to assist with the root-harvesting.

Emba smiled at the sight of her two friends working together. Maybe Odolf had finally got over his jealousy. She could see Fred watching the two of them as well, her left eye still twitching like mad.

"There you go," said Odolf at last, shaking soil off the final plant and adding it to the pile. "That's all of them now. I guess this is where we say goodbye then."

Emba wasn't smiling anymore. Her stomach twisted with disappointment and anger as she realised that

Odolf had only offered to help so he could get rid of Merle sooner.

"No!" said Merle, looking worried. "You can't just leave me out here on my own. Please," she begged, glancing back over her shoulder again. "There might be more arachnomercies or mountain lions. Or bounty hunters. Let me come to the crypt with you and look for your belt buckle. I want to help. It's the least I can do."

"Shh, be quiet, Whip," said Emba. The snake was buzzing like crazy. "Of course you can come," she told Merle, before Odolf or Fred could object. "That's if we can find the way in…"

The Petrified Peaks looked *exactly* like the mountain Emba had been dreaming of each night. Did that mean that the rest of the dream would play out the same in real life too, with the secret door waiting for her in the rock wall? Would it magically open when she pressed her hand against it? And would there be a dragon inside, made of discarded bones, beckoning her into the darkness beyond? To a sharpened claw, waiting for her to prick her finger on. Emba reached instinctively for her scaring-off stone as Whip's buzzing grew even louder.

The red crack that appeared in the sky as they came to a weary halt under the dark shadow of the mountain did little to settle her nerves. There'd been no crack in her dreams—it was the whole sky that was red—but that was of little comfort. The crack in the sky was never a good sign. It only appeared when there was danger on the way.

"This is it then," said Odolf, staring up at the mountain's dark dragon spikes silhouetted against the sky. "This is where I finally get my belt buckle back." He seemed more nervous than excited though, now that they were here. "How do we get in?" He turned to Emba as if she'd know the answer.

"The door must be here somewhere," said Merle, feeling along the rockface with her fingers. "What did it look like in your dream, Emba? Were there any clues?"

"No," said Emba, staring at the solid wall of stone in front of her with a slow, sinking feeling. "I landed in front of the mountain and there it was—a clear doorway cut into the rock. It was just there, waiting for me. And then I reached out and touched it with my hand, like this. I remember looking down and seeing fresh scales on my fingers and then…" She stopped, pulling back her hand in surprise as a faint tingling took hold of her fingers. "Woah," she said. "That was weird. Did you feel it too?"

"Feel what?" asked Merle.

"That tingle," said Emba. "It's gone again now." She stared at the back of her hand, half-expecting to see new scales emerging, but her skin stayed smooth and clear.

"Be careful," Fred warned.

But Emba was already touching her fingers to the rock again, a little further along to the right this time. The tingle returned, even stronger than before. She slid her hand back towards the left and the tingle faded again.

"What are you doing?" asked Odolf. He touched his own hand to the rock and frowned. "I can't feel anything."

"I don't know," said Emba. "It's like something inside the mountain is calling to me." She moved her hand to the right, following the tingle as she traced her fingers along the rock. Soon the tingle became a tickle, then a sharp prickling feeling and then…

"Ow!" Emba yelped with pain, jumping back as if she'd been stung. That's exactly what it felt like—like she'd plunged her fingers into a nest of nip-gnats or pinchworms. But there were no nibbling nip-gnats, no venomous worms, just a solid wall of rock… except maybe it wasn't solid after all. When Emba looked more closely, she could see a faint vertical crack opening up in front of her. *Two* vertical cracks, joined by a horizontal line just above her head.

"Get back!" hissed Fred. "It might not be safe."

But her warning was lost beneath Merle's excitable cry: "The secret doorway!" Merle whooped. "You found it!"

She was right. It was clearly a doorway now. *Just like in my dream*, Emba thought, touching her hand to the door again. There was no pain this time. No prickling, fizzing sensation in her fingers. Nothing but cold smooth rock against her skin. And when she pushed against the rock, the door opened to reveal a set of stone stairs disappearing down into the dark depths of the mountain.

"Wow!" said Odolf, peering over Emba's shoulder. "That was amazing."

Yes, Emba thought. *Amazing. But also terrifying.* She was thinking of that curved dragon claw waiting for her at the far end of the crypt. She could almost feel it calling to her, pulling her towards the open doorway.

"Come on," said Odolf. "What are we waiting for? Let's go!"

"Wait," called Fred. "Not so fast. We don't know what's down there yet. We don't know if it's safe."

"My belt buckle," said Odolf. "*That's* what's down there. That's what it said in the prophecy."

"Hmm." Fred's eye was still twitching wildly. "That's the *first* part of the prophecy. I'm more concerned with the second half and the sleeping forces waking to shake the mountain. I think we should consult the Tome one last time before we go rushing into the unknown," she said, with a sideways glance at Merle. "I've got a funny feeling about this place now that we're finally here. And it's not a good feeling," she added, laying the book down on a nearby rock.

"*I call on you, oh Ancient Tome*," she chanted, as always.

"*To show me what will be,*
Those Terrible Tomorrows
That await inside of thee.
Reveal to me the dreaded course
The cruel Fates have decreed
For she who stands before you now,
Your supplicant in need."

Emba and Odolf had seen the dreadful transformation the Powers of Dreadful Divination wrought on Fred more times than they could count. Merle hadn't though. Emba expected her to be shaken by the sight of Fred's eyes rolling up inside their sockets and the frightful rocking that took hold of her. But she seemed more fascinated than upset, edging even closer for a better view.

"Amazing!" said Merle. "There must be some seriously strong magic inside that book. Can I have a go afterwards?"

But Fred didn't reply. She was already through the dribbling stage and on to the part where her fingers flicked through the Tome's pages at incredible speed, waiting for the right prophecy to reveal itself. And there it was. Fred let out a shuddering gasp as she snatched her hands away from the book and her eyes rolled back into position.

"What does it say?" asked Odolf. "Does it mention anything about my buckle?"

"Does it mention anything about Merle's aunt?" asked Emba.

"Hush now," said Fred, leaning in for a closer look. "*One who seeks will find it there*," she read,

"*Deep inside the hidden lair,*

Buried under rock and stone

With ancient blood and ancient bone.

One who hides will soon reveal

The secret they have come to steal.

Beware the jewel, that ruby red,

That rains destruction on their head."

Odolf was getting impatient. "Well? Is it safe for us to go in or not?" He walked over to the open door in the rock and stared down into the darkness. "The sooner I get my belt buckle, the sooner we can get out of here."

"Hush, Odolf," said Fred. "Let me think."

But Odolf was too impatient to wait. He was already testing out the first step with his foot. Nothing happened. "It seems safe to me," he said as he edged down another step. "Yes, perfectly safe. Don't worry, I promise not to take any rubies, or any other jewels, come to that, so there'll be no rainy destruction coming down on anyone's head. I'll just take my belt buckle and go. The prophecy *says* I'll find it there, so it should be easy enough." He crept down another step. And then another.

"Wait," said Fred. "I'm not sure it's a prophecy about you at all. About any of us. Come back, Odolf."

But it was too late. He'd already gone.

Chapter 21

The Cursed Crypt of Conspiracy

"I'd better go after him," said Emba. "He can't see in the dark like me." *He doesn't know what's waiting inside like I do. He hasn't seen the bones, or the claw...*

Fred touched her hand to her left eye as if to still the frantic twitching. It didn't work though. "I can't let you go down there on your own either," she said, "not after reading that last prophecy. It looks like we're all going," she added, fixing Merle with a strange look. "I just hope I'm wrong."

"Wrong about what?" asked Emba, trying to ignore the prickling under her skin.

Fred was still looking at Merle, who was clutching her aunt's stone like a talisman. "About everything," the old lady said slowly.

"What about the Tome?" asked Emba. "Should we take that with us too? I can carry it if you want."

"Or I can," Merle offered.

Fred shook her head stubbornly. "No, thank you, I'll manage. You take the scrying bowl, Emba. Everything else can stay out here though. We won't be in there long enough to need food or blankets. At least I hope we won't."

Emba tucked the bowl into her bag, alongside her dragon book. "How about you, boy?" she asked Whip. "Are you coming too?"

"Maybe he should wait out here and look after the rest of your things," Merle suggested, but Whip merely buzzed at her. He slithered over to Emba and draped himself back around her neck like a heavy scarf.

"I guess that's a 'yes'," said Emba, secretly rather glad. She felt safer heading into the crypt with a lizard-munching snake for company. "Odolf," she called down the steps as she went. "Wait for us. You won't be able to see where you're going."

"It's fine," came his faint reply. "It's much lighter once you get near the bottom—the ground seems to be glowing. There's no sign of anyone else though. If it *is* a robbers' lair, the robbers must all be out robbing. And there's no sign of my belt buckle either. Or any jewels. I'll keep looking."

"No," Fred told him, wheezing with the weight of the Tome. "Don't touch anything. Don't move. We're coming."

The air grew colder and damper as they headed down the steps into the bowels of the mountain. There was a strange smell too—an old, earthy smell with a tinge of sulphur.

"Are you alright, Fred?" asked Emba, turning to check over her shoulder. "Are you sure you can manage?"

"I'll be fine, Emba dear," said Fred, although she was wheezing harder than ever. "You've got your arms full with Whip. It's you I'm worried about. You never got to tell us the end of your dream. What happened once you got down into the crypt?"

"The bones on the floor turned into a dragon," Emba told her. "A skeleton dragon with a long, hooked claw."

"And was anyone else there in the dream?" asked Merle. "Any *non*-skeleton creatures?"

"No," said Emba. "Just the bone dragon, beckoning me into a swirling darkness at the far end of the crypt. I didn't want to go but I couldn't help myself."

"And then?" asked Fred and Merle together.

"I saw another gleaming claw," Emba told them. "And I pressed my finger to it and—"

"No," interrupted Fred. "Whatever you do, don't start touching any claws. Don't touch anything. Not until we know it's safe."

Emba was at the bottom of the stairs now. The underground chamber looked exactly like the one in her dream except for the bones: there weren't any.

"Why's it so empty?" asked Odolf, who'd stopped to wait for them, as instructed.

"I don't know," said Emba, staring around in confusion.

"And where's my belt buckle? The Tome said it would be waiting here for me to reclaim it, so that I really *will* be Odolf Bravebuckle again. And then when the time comes to fulfil my prophecy—the Final Prophecy, I mean—I'll be ready."

Fred laid a hand on his shoulder, still breathing hard.

"That's not what the Tome meant, Odolf. I'm sorry."

He frowned. "Then what *did* it bring us here for?"

"It's me," Emba murmured, as something at the far end of the crypt caught her eye. Something white and curved and gleaming. A dragon's claw. "I'm the one it wants."

"What are you talking about?" asked Odolf.

Emba didn't reply. She was too busy staring at the claw. Too busy walking towards it as if she was being pulled on an invisible thread. A loud rumbling shook the ground under her feet but she kept on moving.

"Look out!" cried Fred, as an enormous curved bone thrust itself up through the floor to Emba's right, missing her by inches. Emba kept on walking, even as a second giant bone thrust itself up on the left. "Do something, Odolf," Fred begged. "Stop her! But go carefully..."

"Odolf Bravebuckle to the res—Woah! That was a close one. Where are they all coming from?"

Emba was dimly aware of their voices behind her as she walked on:

"They must be the dragon bones from Emba's

dream," Fred was saying. "Be careful."

"It's like they're *trying* to block my path!" answered Odolf. "As soon as I manage to get round one, another bone comes bursting up through the ground, right in front of me!"

"Emba!" That was Fred again. "Stop!"

"Don't listen to them," came Merle's voice. "Keep going, Emba."

She was only dimly aware of Whip's furious buzzing as he tightened his hold on her neck. Only dimly aware of the enormous eyeless skull forcing its way out of the dark earth floor in front of her. Her feet were already changing course, as if by magic, leading her smoothly out of harm's way towards her goal. There was no dark, swirling void waiting for her at the end of the chamber like in her dream though. There was no anything anymore. Just her and the gleaming claw, with a golden chalice underneath to collect her blood. And even though Emba remembered Fred's warning not to touch anything, it felt like the warning belonged to someone else. It belonged to the human side of Emba. But it was the dragon side calling to her now, dragging her towards the waiting claw as if it was her destiny.

As she drew closer, Emba noticed blood-red symbols carved into the rock above. She reached towards them instinctively, trying to make sense of the strange shapes and squiggles. They looked almost like…

"Words," she murmured, feeling something sharpen and shift behind her eyes as she made contact with the rock. Yes, that was better. The carving looked like proper writing now. A proper message:

Only one of dragon kin
Can find the knowledge held within.

"He's here," came Merle's cry from behind. "It's time. Put your finger on the claw, Emba, like in your dream." But Merle's voice seemed little more than a dream now. It *all* felt like a dream.

"No, Emba!" called Fred. "Don't do it."

There was a muffled grunt of effort from behind, followed by a rather less muffled cry of triumph. "There, that's better! It'll take more than a few dragon bones to stop Odolf Bravebuckle. Don't worry, Fred, I'll stop her!"

"Don't you dare!" came Merle's angry response.

Emba was vaguely aware of a scuffle and the sound of someone hitting the floor. But she didn't turn round to see who it was. She was already reaching her hand towards the claw as a trance. It felt as if everything had been leading up to this one single point in her life. She couldn't have stopped even if she wanted to. This was her fate. Her future.

Emba pressed her finger onto the sharpened tip of the claw and watched, mesmerised, as her blood trickled down into the waiting chalice.

There was a sudden, blinding light followed by a muddled chorus of voices all calling at once. Emba couldn't hear what they were saying anymore though. She was too busy staring at the rocky walls and ceiling, at the blood-red writing etching itself into solid stone. So many strange new words. So many long-buried secrets. Even as she stood there, gazing up in wonder, she felt a matching rush of light and strange words—of ancient knowledge—inside her own head, her mind swelling up like a pulsing puff bug. But it was too much already. Too bright. Too noisy. Too disorientating. Emba shut her eyes against the fierce light and the frantic chorus of voices from behind, trying to make sense of what was happening to her. And then a single cry tore through the confusion.

"EMBA!" It was Fred, her voice cracking with fear.

Emba opened her eyes again to see a towering dragon shadow filling the wall in front of her. She gasped as the shadow raised itself up on its mighty dragon legs. She swung round, her heart hammering in her chest, and came face to face with...

...a lizard. A tiny, green lizard rearing up on its little lizard legs, cradled in the outstretched palm of a burly-looking henchman.

Chapter 22

The Crumbling Crypt of Catastrophe

Whatever strange, hypnotic spell had drawn Emba to the dragon's claw and the carved writing was broken now. The dragon bones had stopped pushing up through the ground too, as if they were part of the same peculiar magic. They stood like a windswept forest of fossilised trees, their hard white trunks fixed at strange angles. But there was no wind in the crypt. No sound. No movement. An ominous stillness hung over everything as Emba stared back across the bone-strewn crypt in horror.

"Necromalcolm!" she gasped, finally finding her voice.

"My dragon blood!" squeaked her tiny lizard father.

"That's my belt buckle you're wearing!" yelled Odolf, pointing at Necromalcolm's henchman. It certainly *looked* like his buckle. Emba didn't like to think about what had happened to the horse thieves who'd stolen it from Odolf. Nothing good, she guessed. But Odolf didn't stop to think at all. He was already charging back across the crypt, head down like a raging bull, zigzagging round the giant bones as he ran. "Give it back!"

"Oof!" The henchman was flung back into the wall as the full force of Odolf's skull made contact with his belly. His hands flew up—too late—to protect himself, sending Necromalcolm flying through the air.

A second henchman, identical to the first except for his belt buckle, stepped neatly out of the shadows to save his master, catching his tail in his big, meaty fist. It wasn't much of a rescue though. "Owww! Let go, you dunderhead," Necromalcolm squealed, "before you pull my tail off!" The henchman did as he was told, and the lizard necromancer dropped to the ground like a stone.

Whip uncoiled himself from Emba's neck and slithered down onto the floor after him, fangs bared, buzzing for all he was worth, only for Merle to kick him smartly out of the way.

"Don't even *think* about it!" she cried. "You leave him alone."

The wasp snake recoiled in pain and fell quiet.

"Merle! What are you doing?" Emba demanded, scooping Whip up in her arms. "That's *him!*" she explained. "That's my wicked necromancer dad."

"Merle!" echoed Necromalcolm. "Forget about the snake. Get the chalice." At least that's what it sounded like to Emba, although his voice was so quiet and squeaky it was hard to be sure. And there was no time to puzzle out *why* he'd say something like that to Merle because everything seemed to be happening at once. Odolf had tackled the semi-conscious belt-wearing henchman to the floor and was now trying to wrestle his precious buckle back. Merle, meanwhile, had ignored Emba's warning and was heading for the chalice, just as Necromalcolm had ordered her to. And Fred? Fred was hobbling across the crypt with the Tome of Terrible Tomorrows, ready to swat the lizard and end his wicked plans once and for all.

But Necromalcolm had one more order left to

deliver, cupping his tiny claws to his mouth to make himself heard. "You," he squeaked at a third henchman, who'd appeared out of the shadows as if by magic. "Take care of the old woman."

A single blow was all it took. Emba's guardian was on the floor, groaning, before she could react. And then Odolf was there, his precious belt buckle forgotten in his rush to help Fred. But the henchman was too quick. Too strong. A second shove sent Odolf flying sideways, crashing into the crypt wall with a sickening crunch. He let out a howl of pain and slumped to the floor, his right arm dangling at a strange angle. The henchman wasn't finished with him yet though. Grunting loudly, he tugged a huge, heavy-looking bone out of the ground and laid it down over Odolf's body, pinning him to the spot.

"No! Let me go!" Odolf whimpered, tears of pain—or frustration—running down his cheeks as he attempted to wriggle out from underneath it. But the bone was the perfect fit, with the knobbly ends resting on the ground to keep him from being crushed and the middle section sitting snug against his stomach and chest, trapping him firmly in place.

Emba didn't know who to try and help first: Fred or Odolf. But then Fred made the decision for her.

"Grab the chalice and run," she told Emba, clutching at her heart, her voice cracked and feeble.

"Too late," cried Merle, as Emba turned back towards the cup. She was already holding the golden chalice aloft. "*I've* got the dragon blood now."

"No, Merle," Fred gasped. Her breath sounded ragged and weak. "You have to put it back before it's too late. Remember the prophecy...

Beware the jewel, that ruby red,

That rains destruction on their head.

The ruby red jewel is Emba's blood," Fred explained, her voice little more than a broken whisper as Emba squeezed her way between two jutting rib bones, in pursuit of Merle and the chalice. "If you try and steal it, you'll rain destruction down on us all," Fred warned. There was a loud cracking sound from above, right on cue.

But Merle took no notice. She was too busy picking her way across the bone-littered floor towards

Necromalcolm, who was safely back in his henchman's cupped hands. "Here it is, Uncle," she said, holding the chalice out to him. "Now you *have* to make me your heir."

"*Uncle?*" repeated Emba, coming to an abrupt halt. "What do you mean?" Merle's uncle was dead. Wasn't he? "Wait, *Necromalcolm's* your uncle?"

"That's right, *cousin*," said Merle, her face hardening into a sneer as she turned round to face Emba. "And once he drinks your blood, he'll be back to his full glory." She flinched as a lump of rock came crashing down from the ceiling, missing her by inches.

A second lump of rock landed beside Emba and she leapt back in fright, her hands shooting up to protect her head. The prophecy was coming true already, destruction raining down on them from above. And Merle... Merle must be the duchess's daughter, she realised, jerking sideways to avoid another falling rock. Odolf had spotted the similarity between them, but Emba had been too stubborn to see it. She'd been too busy looking for the good in her new friend to listen to her old friend, or to Fred's worried warnings.

She yelped as a smaller, sharper shard of stone landed beside her, missing her bare foot by inches. She'd been too busy thinking about Merle to see that one coming. Too busy replaying the story about the sick aunt and the curewell roots, which were clearly nothing but lies. Everything about Merle had been a lie, including the stone charm she kept talking to. That must have been how she was communicating with Necromalcolm. They must have been plotting together this whole time. And it was probably *his* magic that kept Merle safe from the sleep-suckers...

I should have listened to Odolf, thought Emba, staring after Merle in shocked betrayal. For a few moments that was all she *could* do: stand there, staring, as the wild flurry of thoughts rushed on through her mind. *It must have been Merle who poisoned Whip as well, to stop him chasing after lizards. Odolf was right about that too. And now he's hurt and trapped and it's all my fault.* She wanted to drag away the heavy bone holding him down, throw her arms around his neck and tell him how sorry she was for doubting him, but her legs seemed to have forgotten how to move. She felt as rooted to the spot as Necromalcolm had been when they first met. The thought of the roof caving in on Odolf as she stood there like a statue finally kicked her body back into action though. She had to stop Necromalcolm getting his lizard claws on that chalice. She had to return it to its rightful place beneath the dragon claw, otherwise they were all doomed.

Blood pounded in Emba's ears as she set off again, taking a sharp right turn at a towering thigh bone, determined to reach the lizard necromancer before it was too late. But she wasn't the only one with her sights set on her father.

"Whip, come back!" The wasp snake was off again, slithering to the floor and shooting off towards Necromalcolm, buzzing as he went. Emba lurched after him. "No!" she cried, as a fourth henchman stepped out of the shadows, scooping the snake up in his big, hairy hands and knotting him round a jutting dragon bone like a piece of old rope. And when Whip started wriggling and writhing to try and free himself, the henchman pulled back his meaty fist and punched him on the nose. The wriggling stopped and the snake's head slumped back down to the floor.

"No!" Emba cried again, her dragon's blaze raging inside her belly. But she forced herself to swallow it back down as an entire section of ceiling collapsed in a shower of rocks. They were in enough trouble already, without setting fire to anything. Or *anyone*. The dragon part of her might have taken over for a while, but the human part of her was back in control now. And humans didn't go around setting fire to other humans—or lizards—no matter how evil they were. Not even when one of the evil lizard's henchmen was tipping a vial of frothing, pungent green liquid, into the chalice with the stolen blood. *No, no, no!*

"STOP!" she roared, throwing herself at the chalice a second time, hoping to knock the hissing, foaming contents onto the floor. But it was too late. *She* was too late. Lizard Necromalcolm was already squeaking his strange magic words over the mixture, as the other henchman caught Emba in his mighty arms, pinning her to the spot. And suddenly, he wasn't *lizard* Necromalcolm anymore. He was a writhing mass of torn green scales and bulging bones, of bubbling skin and thrashing limbs that seemed to grow and stretch before Emba's very eyes. Fresh beard hairs sprouted out of his chin as he let out a dark, evil laugh, setting off an even bigger rockfall. The crypt seemed to be cracking and crumbling around them as Necromalcolm transformed back from reptile to man.

"At last!" he cried, throwing up his human arms in triumph. Or maybe he was just lifting them up ready for the *fifth* identical henchman stepping out of the shadows clutching a spare necromancer's robe. He slipped it on over his master's head and the transformation was complete. Necromalcolm's skin was still a little green, with a few loose scales glistening in his beard, but other than that he was his old self again.

"No!" Emba struggled uselessly against her captor's steely grip.

"Yes!" crowed Necromalcolm. "I can feel my full magic starting to return. And the power of flight will soon be mine too."

"That's brilliant, Uncle," said Merle, her dark eyes shining as she stared up at him. "And now you've got your body back, you can make me your heir like you promised." A large crack opened up above her head, but she didn't seem to notice. She was too busy reminding Necromalcolm of everything she'd done to deliver Emba back into his clutches. "I even poisoned the snake in case it tried to eat you—that was my own idea—but Emba saved it with her magic. Her powers are wasted on her though. I'll make a *much* better heir. I can look after everything down here for you, while you're conquering the dragon realm."

"We'll see," said Necromalcolm. "Do you still have the stone I entrusted to you?"

"Yes," said Merle, handing him the grey stone with the hole through the middle. "It's right here. Did it work? Could you hear me talking to you through it?"

"Yes, I heard you," said Necromalcolm. "You did well. But I have another need for it now. There are secrets here—an ancient knowledge written into the very walls themselves. My dragon powers are not yet strong enough to decipher them, but they will be. Oh yes, they will be. And when the great day finally arrives—when the breach between the two realms opens once more—I'll be ready to seize my place as the master of all. The *immortal* master of all."

Emba tried kicking her way to freedom, her bare feet pummelling at the henchman's legs as another large lump of rock came crashing down to her right. It might be too late to stop Necromalcolm, but it wasn't too late to save her friends. The henchman simply laughed though, as if she was nothing more than a ticklish insect, and held her out at arm's length instead.

Odolf, meanwhile, had somehow managed to squeeze himself out from underneath the giant bone. Emba see him crawling over to Fred, one-handed, and putting his ear to her mouth as if to check she was still breathing. *Please tell me she's still breathing.* And then he was pushing himself up onto his feet again, his face contorted with pain and anger, as he staggered towards Necromalcolm with a raw cry of fury. Showers of falling rocks bounced at his feet as he ran, dodging and twisting.

"Don't worry, Uncle, I'll get him," cried Merle, leaping forwards to tackle him. But henchman number three—or was it number four?—was quicker, scooping Odolf up like a sack of flour and tossing him over his shoulder.

Odolf whimpered in pain, his bad arm swinging limply beneath him. But he still found the strength to hammer his other fist against the henchman's big, burly back. His captor seemed as oblivious to Odolf's desperate pummelling as he was to the fragments of rock bouncing down on his head though. He was too busy staring at Necromalcolm, as the necromancer thrust the grey, holed stone up into the air, muttering strange, hissing words under his breath.

The hole at the stone's centre began sucking the brightness out of the room as if it was drinking it in—drinking in the light and the blood-red words on the walls—and swallowing up the last of Emba's hopes. She didn't understand what was happening, but she knew it was bad. Very bad. Necromalcolm had finally completed his spell. He'd taken her dragon blood—blood that had been freely given this time—and the first part of his plan was complete. Now he was stealing the knowledge she'd unleashed—the same ancient knowledge that had burned itself into her brain—and there was nothing anyone could do to stop him. Not her, not Odolf or Whip and definitely not Fred, who lay quiet and still. Why wasn't she moving?

"Hurry, Uncle," shouted Merle, as another section of ceiling collapsed behind them. "We'll be crushed if we don't get out of here soon."

Necromalcolm nodded. "It's done," he declared, as the last of the light disappeared into the stone, plunging the crypt into darkness. But only for a moment. Necromalcolm clicked his fingers and a swarm of torch bugs appeared out of nowhere, their glowing wings lighting up the crypt once more. "I have everything I came for now. The prophecy is—"

He broke off as a terrible roar tore through the air: *Let her go!*

Emba didn't just *hear* it, she felt it too—felt the power of the words thrilling through her entire body.

"Who said that?" asked Necromalcolm, swinging round in shock. "Where are you?"

"Who said what?" asked Merle. "I didn't hear anything."

"That voice," said Necromalcolm. "That terrible, wonderful voice."

There was a thunderous beating noise and Emba's dragon mother came swooping down into the crypt like a giant winged ghost, straight through the solid rock ceiling. A ceiling that was getting *less* solid with every passing minute. Another shower of rock followed her down to the floor as she opened up her enormous, smoking jaws and called out again: *Let her go!*

"I can hear you," gasped Emba, staring up into her mother's huge, scaled face. It wasn't merely a roar. Those were words. Proper words. *It must be the dragon knowledge*, she thought. *It's inside me now.*

Necromalcolm pointed to the henchman holding Emba. "Do as she says," he ordered, his dark eyes glinting with excitement. Or was it fear? "Let the girl go... for now. My powers are not yet strong enough to take on a dragon—to defy the new dragon blood inside of me. They will be, though," he added, turning back to Emba's mother with a hiss. "When the great day comes, there'll be no stopping me. And it's coming... it's coming soon."

"A dragon?" said the henchman, releasing his hold on Emba. "What dragon?"

"That one there, you blithering fool," shouted Necromalcolm, cowering as a fearsome burst of flame filled the crypt. "The one with the dragon's blaze!" But it was clear to Emba that her mother and her fire were as invisible to the henchman as they were to everyone else. Everyone except for Necromalcolm. He must be able to see them too now, thanks to the dragon's blood he'd swallowed. And thanks to the magic stone clutched in his hand, he must be able to understand her mother's roars as well. Whatever ancient dragon knowledge had burned its way into Emba's mind was now inside the stone too.

The wall above the curved claw shook.

The ceiling trembled.

"Time to go," said Necromalcolm, grabbing Merle by the elbow. "Your mother will never forgive me if you end up buried under a pile of rocks. Bring the belt-buckle thief with you as protection," he added, turning back to Odolf's captor. "The girl won't risk using her dragon's blaze on us so long as we've got him."

"No!" Emba screamed, a fresh tunnel of rage burning up inside her as she watched her best and only friend get carted off. Necromalcolm was right though. She couldn't risk using her flames. And she couldn't leave Fred.

"Put me down," Odolf yelled as the henchman carried him straight through the belly of Emba's dragon mother, towards the stone steps. "No one kidnaps Odolf Bravebuckle!" But courage and determination were no match for sheer brute strength. No matter how hard Odolf kicked and punched and wriggled, the henchman kept on walking.

"I'll find you, Odolf!" Emba called after them. "I promise. I—" But she never got to finish her sentence. She never got to apologise for not believing him. Never got to tell him how much he meant to her. There was a terrible, terrifying rumble that shook the very air around her. And then Odolf disappeared altogether as the crypt ceiling finally caved in.

Chapter 23

The Abysmal End of Everything

"Odolf!" Emba screamed.

"Emba!" came a faint, echoing cry from the other side of the wall—a new wall of fallen rock and stone that blocked off any last sliver of hope Emba had of saving her friend, along with any chance of getting out of the crypt in one piece. She was trapped. So was Fred, and Whip too—if he was still alive.

"Wait!" came a new cry from the other side of the wall. It sounded like Merle. "What about Emba? How will she get out? And Fred?"

Necromalcolm laughed a low, bitter laugh. "What about them? I have everything I need now. Emba's no use to me anymore."

"But she's your daughter," Merle said.

"She *was* my daughter," Necromalcolm snapped. "I offered to give her everything and she threw it back in my face. She blasted me into my own cauldron and reduced me to a simpering reptile. But now I have a new heir ready and waiting to do my bidding. This is what you wanted, after all."

"Yes, I know," said Merle. "But…" Her voice trailed away into the distance. Emba waited for them to come back. Waited for her father to change his mind.

She waited, too shocked to move.

And waited, staring at the wall of fallen stone until her eyes stung. Until tears rolled down her cheeks and dripped off the end of her chin.

Hush now, came a low, velvety voice in her ear.

Fred? Emba span round in confusion, wondering what had happened to her guardian's voice. But it wasn't Fred. It was the dragon.

Hush, she said again. *He hasn't won quite yet. There's still a chance.*

"Yes," said Emba, wiping her eyes on the back of her hand. "*You* can go after him." Stone walls were nothing to her mother while she was in her spirit form.

"You need to stop Necromalcolm before he gets his powers back. You need to save Odolf and Fred…"

The old lady still hadn't moved. Emba hurried over to her side. "Fred! Fred, are you alright? Can you hear me?" Fred's eyes were closed, her hand clutched to her chest. "Wake up. Please wake up." Emba held her fingers to her guardian's mouth. She was still breathing, but only just.

Emba turned back to her mother. "We have to help her. We have to *do* something."

The dragon's large milky eyes filled with tears. *There's nothing you can do for her now. Her days in this realm have come to an end.*

"No," sobbed Emba. "It's not her time. Not yet." The thought of waving her beloved guardian off to the afterlife was too terrible to even consider. Fred belonged in *this* realm. The realm of the living. Unless… "What if you were to take her back to *your* realm?" asked Emba, remembering what she'd read in the book Howard had given her about the dragons' source of immortality. That's what Necromalcolm was after too, wasn't it? Emba knew the breach wouldn't open to mortals until her birthday, but there was little mortal life *left* in her guardian now. Her mother could fly Fred back through the red crack with *her*. Couldn't she? "The dragons can help her. I know they can. You have to take her with you."

Emba's mother shook her head. *I'm not strong enough for that. Not in my spirit form. It would take ten dragons to carry her from this realm to ours.*

"Then we need to find another nine," said Emba, gritting her teeth with determination. "Please," she begged. "You're my mother. And so's Fred—she's looked after me all these years. You have to help her."

Dark times are coming, child, said the dragon, sadness swimming in her eyes, *and this will only make things harder for you.*

"I don't care," said Emba with a strangled sob. "Whatever it takes. Just do it. Please."

The dragon closed her eyes and sighed a deep, rumbling sigh. *Very well,* she said at last, touching the misty tip of her snout to the top of Emba's head. There was nothing there to feel—no flesh, no bone— and yet Emba felt it all the same. She felt a fierce rush of something warm and urgent burning into her. And then it was gone again, as her mother threw back her mighty head and roared.

There were no words this time, just a terrible, ear-splitting roar that shook Emba to her bones. And then came the flame: a pure green flame that burned into the crypt wall, melting the stone away as if it was nothing but ice. Emba could see daylight through the hole now—a pale shaft of sunlight that came streaming into the ruins of the mountain crypt, bringing a fresh beam of hope with it, and the sound of beating wings.

Another dragon, thought Emba, as a second ghostly beast came flapping down through the red crack in the sky, with another one following behind it. And another. And another… Soon there was nothing but dragons, of every shape and size, from huge horn-nosed beasts with fearsome spiked tails to a smooth-spined creature with four heads, their spectral outlines filling the sky. Down they came, one after the other, ignoring the hole and flying straight through the rocky walls and ceiling to land beside Fred, weaving soft plumes of silver smoke around her body like a cradle.

Ten dragons to carry one little old lady to safety. To carry her back to life.

We don't have long, said Emba's mother. *She's fading fast.*

Emba nodded, flinging herself down beside her guardian and kissing her cheek. "Goodbye, Fred," she whispered. "I love you."

Chapter 24

The Epilogue After the End of Everything

Emba Oak stared up at the sky as her beloved guardian was carried away through the red crack, cradled in silver smoke, to the dragon realm beyond. But her eyes were too misty with tears to see.

"Oh Fred," she whispered into the eerie stillness, as the sound of the dragons' wings faded away to nothing. "What will I do without you?"

There was no answer. The red crack lingered for a moment more, then sealed itself closed again and disappeared.

Emba sank down onto her knees as the tears gathered force down her cheeks. She'd never felt as lost and lonely as she did now. Fred was gone. Odolf was gone. Her dragon mother was gone. Even

Whip was gone—there was no sign of him anywhere. *Everyone* was gone. There was nobody left to stop Necromalcolm from ascending into the dragon realm when the breach between their world and this one opened up on her twelfth birthday. No one to stop him seizing power: power over the earth and power over the skies. And power over life itself. Yes, once he had the secret of immortality in his grasp, he'd be invincible.

"No," said a voice in Emba's head. A little whispering voice. "There *is* someone who can stop him."

Emba took no notice. She carried on weeping.

But the voice hadn't finished with her yet.

"It's not over yet," it said, a little louder than before. "*You* can stop him."

Emba shook her head. No, it was too late. He was too powerful.

"You can stop him," insisted the voice. "You can find Odolf. You can stop Necromalcolm. *You* can be the hero from the Final Prophecy."

The Final Prophecy? Emba wiped her tears on the back of her hand. And then wiped her nose on the back of her other hand, as she replayed the words of the Tome of Terrible Tomorrow's Final Prophecy in her mind:

A hero forged in fiercest flame,
A child of iron and pain
By blood shall heal and chasm seal
A kingdom torn in twain.

What if the voice inside her head was right? What if *she* was the hero forged in fiercest flame, not Odolf? What if the flames were nothing to do with a blacksmith's forge, as Odolf had always believed? What if they were *dragon* flames?

Emba took a deep breath and pulled herself up off the ground. The voice in her head was right. She had to save Odolf. She had to stop Necromalcolm. And she had to believe that Fred was going to be alright— that the dragons would save her and Emba would find her again somehow. But before she did any of that, she had to rescue the Tome of Terrible Tomorrows. That's what Fred would have wanted.

Emba crawled back through the hole in the wall into the ruins of the dragon bone crypt, searching the rubble for the abandoned book. Sharp edges of rock cut at her fingers as she scrabbled through the wreckage, but she refused to give up. *It has to be here somewhere.*

Buzzzzzzzzz.

What was that?

Emba held her breath as she stopped to listen.

Buzzzzzzzzzzz.

"Whip? Is that you?" She frantically followed the buzzing sound to a piece of dragon skull, peeking out from under a large pile of stones, praying that he'd managed to unknot himself and find shelter from the collapsing ceiling. "It's alright, boy, I'm coming," she said, tossing the stones off one at a time. "I'll get you out of there. Don't worry." The more stones Emba moved, the louder the buzzing became, until at last she caught a glimpse of yellow and black scales peeking through the skull's hollow eye hole.

"Oh Whip," she cried as the wasp snake slithered free to meet her. "I thought I'd lost you too." There were more tears running down her cheeks now, but these were happy tears. Hopeful tears. "I'm not on my own anymore," she whispered to the snake, touching her hand to the cool smoothness of his scales. "We just need to find the Tome of Terrible Tomorrows and then... and then we'll go and save Odolf." It sounded like a plan when she said it like that. A frightening, dangerous, almost-impossible plan, but a plan nevertheless.

"Wait, where are you going?" she asked as Whip slithered away across the floor. "Come back," she cried, chasing after him. He stopped beside another pile of stones, with the curved spike of a dragon rib sticking out of the top. And there it was: the Tome of Terrible Tomorrows. Emba picked it up and blew away the thin layer of dust that had settled over the eight-legged monster on the front cover. That was part one of her plan taken care of already.

"Well done, boy," she said as the snake wrapped himself, purring, around her neck. "Thank you."

Emba Oak and her wasp snake crawled back out through the hole in the wall and stood looking up at the sky. Somewhere up there beyond the gathering clouds—beyond the very edges of the human world— were Fred and Emba's dragon mother. Emba tipped back her head, opened her mouth, and sent a fierce beam of flame up towards the heavens. And then she reached into her bag for her trusty scaring-off stone and smiled.

"Now to find Odolf and save the world," she said.

The End